LIVE TO IMAGINE

Anthology of Award-winning Short Stories

ISBN-13: 978-0-9742652-2-3
ISBN-10: 0-9742652-2-5

DEDICATION

This anthology is dedicated to those who live to imagine

To the authors featured in this book: Scribes Valley thanks you for
your time, patience, trust, and talent.

CONTENTS

LIVE TO IMAGINE
A Foreword by David L. Repsher, editor

*Heavy wind swept across the clearing, howling through the
surrounding maples and pounding the tiny cabin with sheets of
rain as the worn and bent farmer trudged across the newly-sown
lawn, making for the warmth of the candle-lit windows.*

Did you get a mental picture as you read the above sentence?
Did you see the cabin? Did you see the rain blowing across the
clearing and beating on the tiny structure?

If you answered yes, consider yourself extremely lucky. You
have retained your imagination. You can see beyond the obvious.
You have enough mind control to let your mind be uncontrolled.
You can leave the everyday world and visit other worlds whenever
you want to.

If you answered no, if you saw only words on a page, go ahead
and make your reservation at the Home for the Imaginationally
Challenged. You are a prisoner in your own brain. Your mind is
doomed to stay locked inside. You are dead from the neck up. You
need help!

We are all born with an imagination. It starts with the first
intrusion of light into our newborn eyes, and then begins to grow
and mature as we grow and mature.

At least, it's *supposed* to.

Let's do a little unscientific (*very* unscientific) study on the
imagination and how a normal one develops (or should develop).

Imagination/Age Development Study 2005

Age: birth to one year

The imagination is small, very small. In fact, it's barely there. That's okay, though, because it doesn't take much to suck in food and fill a diaper. Since everything is done for you, your brain can chill out and spoon feed the imagination from the ambience of the strange new world called Life.

Age: one to five years

The imagination is awake now and starting to kick in, noticing everything and coming up with ideas. It has also developed a voice, with which it communicates directly with its host. Things like:

"Oatmeal is nature's paint, kid, and just look how plain the dining room walls are!"

"I bet worms taste like chicken."

"Dogs really enjoy mud baths."

"Aw, just pretend you still have a diaper on and LET IT FLY!"

"Sucker, shmucker, RUN!"

Age: six to ten years

It's still talking, but coming up with bigger and better ideas, complete with a sick sense of humor:

"Things live in the closet. It's so slopping over with things that some of them had to move out to live under the bed."

"The things in the attic are wimps compared to the things in the basement!"

"Was that a thing looking in the window just now?"

But it's not all scary. The imagination is now the strongest it will ever be. Familiar objects start to take on new forms. A simple cardboard box becomes a police car, a space rocket, a time machine, a test capsule for cat-down-the-stairs experiments...

Backyards turn into steaming jungles full of wild beasts just waiting to be tamed and carted off to a zoo somewhere.

And, the entire world is crawling with bad guys to conquer:

"Uh, oh! Fifty ninjas in sight, and that's just the ones on the roof!"

"Hungry dinosaurs attacking over the back fence, get ready to fight!"

"Man, good thing this gun never runs out of bullets, or we'd all have to learn to speak Martian."

Age: eleven to fifteen years

The imagination is getting some major competition now, from electronics. Video games and computer games bombard the brain so fast and hard, there's no time to check in on the imagination. Why make up your own fantasies when some programmer has already thought them up for you?

But, through all the bleeps, blips, crashes, and explosions, the voice of the imagination still manages to come through.

"Dinner? Dinner can wait until the high score is shattered."

"Can't even think about bedtime before the next level is achieved."

"Time has lost all meaning. Clocks don't even tick-tock anymore."

The imagination at this point even has the power to override bodily function signals.

<u>**WARNING WARNING WARNING**</u>
BLADDER FLUID LEVELS REACHING CRITICAL MASS
SPHINCTER MUSCLES LOOSENING
WET PANTS IMMINENT

"No problem, the bladder can expand to fifty times its normal size. Keep playing!"

Toward the end of this age period, the imagination gets a bit cruel and directs the attention downward to the body. The body that's changing.

"Where'd that hair come from? Good grief, next thing you

know, you'll be howling at the full moon."

"Hey! Things are suddenly growing down there. Call 911!"

Age: sixteen to twenty years

The electronic noise is replaced by the sound of hormones ricocheting around inside the brain pan. Something called puberty makes an appearance and the imagination gets renewed attention. Its voice is much louder and a bit more inventive.

"Hey, look at that! Isn't that the person who gave you the creeping cooties just last week? Not bad now, eh?"

"Hmm...those kissing scenes in the movies used to turn your stomach, but it might not be so bad now. Maybe you should try it..."

Also, at this time, the imagination decides body quality is one of the most important things.

"Holy cow! Is that a zit or did someone build a mountain on your face last night?"

"Better smear that deodorant on all the way from armpit to hip. Remember the sweat stains that appeared at the party last week?"

"Your feet are too big."

"Your hands are too big."

"Your nose is too big."

"Your IQ is too small."

Age: twenty-one to forty

The body no longer needs so much attention. Other things take over and steer the imagination toward such concerns as:

"Shouldn't you have been married by now? Everybody else is."

"Settle down, buy a house, have kids, get a mortgage, get an ulcer."

"You call that a salary? Homeless people are making more than you are!"

"Say, isn't that cute young thing over there flirting with you?"

Age: forty-one to...sixty

The imagination is getting older now and becoming a friend once again.

"Sure, you can get out and play with the kids for hours! Yeah, you can keep up. You're just as quick as they are and they'll benefit from your wisdom."

"Aw, who needs extra sleep? You can live on only three hours sleep a night. Refill that popcorn bowl and find yourself another movie."

"Walk a little slower and let that cute young thing over there get a good, lingering shot of your butt."

"Go ahead, flaunt your maturity. It's what everybody hopes to achieve one day."

Age: sixty-one to...the end

Rather than spend time thinking up new ideas and things to try, the imagination turns on you once again and fires off little self-degrading quips about the body's abilities.

"Start wheezing louder and maybe somebody will come and carry you up these steps."

"Uh-oh! Let's hope that popping noise right then wasn't a hip."

"Oh, is that another wrinkle? Hmm...Didn't think a person could wrinkle there!"

"Liver spots? But, you hate liver."

"Either your gray hair is turning white, or somebody's gluing cotton balls to your head while you sleep."

"Okay, you've finally made it to the living room, and there's your favorite chair, but you need the bathroom again. Right now!"

End of Report

So, as you can see, your imagination dictates how you live your life and how you see the world. And it's always been there to see you through the tough times, trials, and tribulations.

Don't believe me? Well, how many times did you make it

through some boring school class by letting your imagination take you away? How many times did you reduce your parents' scolding voices to the level of crickets on a hot summer night while your mind was in the next galaxy? How many times have you answered your significant other's personal questions—not with what you really felt—but with what you thought they wanted to hear?

Yes, your imagination can be your best friend. But, unfortunately, society sometimes frowns on those who use their imaginations frequently. An imaginative person is unkindly described as "daydreamer," "aloof," "withdrawn," "shy," "backward," "weird."

On the other hand, those of us in the know might call such a person "inventor," "scholar," "scientist," "author."

So, use your imagination every day. Let it soar to new heights. Let it seek out new adventures and new ideas

Live to experience all you can experience. Live to see the world through open eyes and an open mind. Live to realize there are no boundaries to your imagination.

Live...to imagine

POETRY
FIRST PLACE

HE

Maybe today
when the phone rings
it will be him
and the music
of his words
will wrap around me
the same way
his arms
used to
so many
months
ago

Maybe tonight
when I close my eyes
to dream
I will see him
and we will dance
so closely
that the rhythm
of my pulse
will join with his
and flow
like a river
to the ocean

Maybe tomorrow
as I struggle
through the day
I will skim

the surface
of the stream
my tears have cried
without drowning
in the salty bitterness
of the wake
he has
left behind

Maybe one day
soon
he will call
with the news
that he
is coming home
and I will leap
into his arms
as he swings me
around and around
under the smiling
September sun

Maybe then
after my lips
have found his
we will kiss
and I will twist
my tongue so far
into his heart
that I can taste
his love
and smell
his sweet soul
and I'll dive so deep
into everything
that is him
that I needn't
come up
for air
because
he
is my
breath

STAND

The steel blade of
Resentment,
Its handle too hot
To hold
Carves its way into
My being
And melts its signature
On the back of
My heart

A frothy cup of
Uncertainty
Brought to my lips,
Its bitterness
Unaffected
By the heaping teaspoons
Of sugar
I add
And add

The promise of
Hope
Whispered anonymously
In my ear
And felt when the sun
Cradles my face
In the warmth of
Its hands;

And it smiles
Knowingly
For it sees that
Wisdom
Takes so long
To attach its roots
To the side
Of a soul
And grow like ivy

LIVE TO IMAGINE

On a Harvard
Brick wall

While Peace lies
Waiting
On its hands and knees
In a corner
Of a forest
Of fear
And, Peace crouches
In the corner
Paralyzed
Trembling
Terrified to stand

MILES

2001 by Jean B. Speights

He pedals along
the edge
of an Interstate
Oblivious
Pearls of sweat
leap
from his face
leaving freckles of rust
between the battered spokes

His mismatched socks
pulled up high
above his calves
The material molded
to his muscles
shaped by his travels
every day
determined
to reach his destination
of a location unknown

Scanty branches
stretched out
their thin shadows
of shade
offering little
sanctuary
as Heat's cruel hands
reach up
through the pavement
and iron
another wrinkle
in the fabric
of his face

In my Mercedes-Benz
the climate
comfortable
Watching

stationary
Six lanes of
five o'clock Friday
gridlock
Powerless
loosening my tie
Cell phone
Static
losing sight of
the man
on the bicycle

It is then
that I realize
with a
cocked head
and a curious
Smile
that this rusty
old man
with his world
strapped to his back
and no shoes
upon his feet
is Miles ahead
Of us all

About the Author:

Jean grew up in Ithaca, New York, but currently resides in Poqouson, Virginia, on the Chesapeake Bay, with her Special Forces husband, who travels extensively, and their 10-year-old twin girls, who are both creative, artistic, and straight-A students. She has always loved to "fool around and write" in her spare time, as a child and as an adult. Her high school and college English teachers encouraged her to pursue writing. She wound up going to court reporting school and became a Merit writer recording, transcribing and editing legal transcripts. Although she has a passion for technical writing, it's not quite as liberating as writing from the heart. Jean's favorite pastimes include decorating, canoeing, tinkering around on the piano, and just reveling in a few moments of peace and quiet, all the while keeping the company of Mozart or Bach, or, perhaps, Bon Jovi, should the moment feel right.

SHORT STORY
FIRST PLACE

NAMES
©2000 by Francis W. Porretto

Census has always been an irritant. There are many—I am one—who feel it to be intrusive, however necessary it might be. And the costs, both to the government and to the individuals it enumerates, should not be discounted.

I have the trust of certain highly placed persons. Because of my reputation for thoroughness and integrity, at the outset of the last two censuses, the tetrarch has assigned me the supervision of a district. I took advantage of this to tell him of the grumblings the census causes. On the first occasion he assured me that the complaints I heard were the braying of asses, nothing more. Census had never caused a revolt and would cause none. This last time he was slower to respond.

On my way back to Jerusalem with my tallies, I decided to take lodging at a country inn rather than travel through the night. The proprietors knew me from previous encounters. Well that it was so, for there was only one room left and a goodly throng clamoring for it. I tried to be unobtrusive about securing it for myself, but a few noticed and protested as vigorously as their fatigue would allow. To avert the disturbance, I slipped out of the common room as quickly and quietly as I could. When I'd divested myself of my bags, I descended the back stairs to wander the hills until my mind had quieted enough to allow me to sleep.

A census marshal has absolute authority over the procedures to be used in his district. Knowing the popular sentiment, I took the inconveniences upon myself. I went from town to town, consulting with local magistrates and figures of prominence, and took the count without requiring anything of the people save their names.

The local officials were always glad to see me go. What would be required of them and their neighbors afterward, of course, was money. Census is always about money: how many folk there are, and how prosperous, and what levy can be exacted of them without provoking an insurrection.

By the size and surliness of the throng on the roads that day, and at the inn, I knew I was passing through a district whose marshal was not so kindly disposed. As the law permitted, he'd ordered the people to come to him. He'd imposed enormous discomfort upon every man of that region, rather than burden himself with the dust and expense of my sort of circuit.

It was not a happy place.

In passing through a crowd, I am forever speculating. Which among these, I ask myself, is known to his neighbors as a person of substance? Which is reviled for his indulgences, or held in contempt for his dissolution? Which among them is known outside his village, and why? Which of them will become known? Which of them, by dint of deeds mighty or monstrous, will climb to stand on the shoulders of history? Which will change our world?

Usually it's a way of passing the dreary times, no more.

The day had provided me with copious fodder. There was an old man in a dirty samite robe, stooped nearly double from years of toil, who leaned so heavily upon his staff as he walked that I feared it might break beneath him. Yet when his wife addressed him in a manner he disapproved, he straightened like a spring suddenly unbound and struck her across the face with that same staff, to send her to the ground bleeding and blubbering. There was a merchant, a large, solid man in a rich cloak of gabardine, who intervened uninvited in a loud dispute between a traveler and a street peddler, to counsel them to moderation. They turned their wrath from one another to him, hurling the foulest of epithets into his face until he left them to resume their profitless quarrel. There was a tall youth of perhaps twenty, with a face of chiseled perfection and a body like unto the Greeks' statues of their gods. He strode smiling through the world as if he owned everything in it, and all marveled at his beauty as he passed. Yet when a raddled old harlot beckoned to him in terms too vulgar even to think them onto this page, he did not respond with derision or scorn. He stopped and went to her, spoke to her softly, pressed a coin into her hand, and passed on.

Of which of these would I hear again? Any? None?

Even if it should happen, I would not know. I did not know their names. My acquaintance with names was a professional one, confined to the tallies I carried in my saddlebags.

The sun had dropped below the horizon, and the hills were growing cold. The traffic on the road to the city had dwindled to nothing. Outside the inn, the stragglers for whom there were no accommodation crouched and huddled against its southern wall, making what provisions they could for a night of unplanned exposure. In the near distance a shepherd surrendered his staff to his son and trudged back to his hovel for an evening meal.

Movers? Shakers? Doers of mighty deeds? Icons of superlative virtue or courage?

Not likely.

Even those acclaimed as such by the world often struck me as persons elevated to their stations by blind chance, rather than merit. One night, deep in his cups, a patrician of my acquaintance admitted as much to me. He called his chamberlain a more able man by far. In a better world, he allowed, their positions would have been reversed. I agreed, though I forbore to say so.

I passed no judgments. I was no mover or shaker. I was a functionary, an industrious keeper of tablets with a gift for inspiring confidence in those of higher station, nothing more. No deed of mine would disturb the world's slumbers. My name would not be recorded in an annal of greatness nor praised from a tall tower.

There was some comfort in it.

The night grew cold. The clouds receded from the southern sky, and the stars brought their pale glory to that humblest of places. I headed back to the inn, with no thoughts but of a mug of mead and an early bed.

A faint commotion arose as I passed the stables. The doors were closed, of course, but human sounds issued from within. I stopped and laid my ear against the wind-worn wood. A woman was panting with increasing urgency. A male voice murmured repeated exhortations to courage.

It climaxed with a great cry, followed by a lesser one: the unmistakable wail of a newborn child. The tallies for that district would be augmented by one.

One what? Shepherd? Peddler? Laborer? Surely not a rich merchant, whose hands would flow with gold and whose path would be strewn with obsequies lifelong. Surely not a prince of the realm, whose stern gaze and unblinking eye would strike fear into lesser men and command them to instant obedience. Not a mover or a shaker. Such were not born in stables.

I swung back the stable door and slipped inside. No one noticed.

There were only the three: man, woman, and child. A single frail candle burned against the back wall of the stable, casting their silhouettes at me like inverted shadows. The woman had wrapped the baby in a loose cocoon of white muslin, leaving only its head exposed, and was laying it in the feed-trough that stood between the rows of stalls. She straightened, stepped back, and wordlessly collapsed into the man's arms.

Around the little tableau, the horses were silent.

I stepped forward, started to address the couple, and stopped. He cradled her in his lap, his arms tight about her, his face ablaze with uxorious devotion. Her eyes, large and luminous, were fixed upon her new child.

It took all my strength to produce a voice. "Do you...require anything?"

Her gaze remained locked upon her child. He assessed me with a glance and nodded with a certainty I could not help but envy.

"Some water, perhaps."

I nodded and started for the inn, but something held me. I bent to the feed-trough, pulled the muslin back from the tiny face and looked into it, not knowing why or what I hoped to see.

The baby's eyes were open.

The eyes of the newborn are never open.

They were large, and dark, yet filled with the light of a million stars, and more knowledge than I had seen in the eyes of any man, high or low. They held recognition and regal acceptance.

I know you for what you are, that infant gaze said. *Without knowing, you have sought me, and now I have come for you, and for all those like you. The humble and the just. Though you know not my name, though it be the least of the tallies for this census, and not even one of yours, when you hear it you will know it at once. On a day not far off I shall summon you, and instruct you in the ways of truth and righteousness, and together we will awaken this weary world to a dawn of hope.*

The eyes closed. I stood and backed away.

"I'll fetch water," I whispered. Neither husband nor wife stirred. I slipped out of the stable and closed the door behind me.

The common room of the inn was crowded and painfully noisy. There were far too many folk there for its size. Servants moved quickly through the room with mugs, plates and coarse blankets, stumbling here and there, receiving muttered thanks or none at all. I stood at the arch to the kitchen and waited to be noticed.

"Is there water?"

A young girl turned away from the pot she was stirring and looked up at a portly man tending a large oven. He nodded. She filled an ewer from a dip well and presented it to me in both hands. I took it and thanked her.

"There's a couple in the stables..."

The man nodded. "We know."

"She's given birth."

"Is she well? And her baby?"

"I think so."

He took a loaf from a high shelf and brought it to me. "We haven't much left. The first harvest won't be soon enough for me. But we do what we can, as little as that may be."

I smiled. "It will serve."

He nodded and returned to his labors.

The family in the stable was as I had left it. The child was asleep. The man accepted the bread and water with grave thanks. He was dividing it with his wife as I left them.

We all do what we can. For some, that is more than for others, but no effort is to be shirked. I was far from my place of resource, but that did not excuse me from my portion.

What of the child in the manger? What would his portion be?

I had met a great one at last. A king of kings, one whose proper place would be at the head of every table.

I hoped I might live to see him rise to his estate, but if I did not, it would be of little moment. I had seen him enter the world. That would be enough.

Jerusalem was a day's ride away. The next day I delivered the census rolls, and remarked again to the tetrarch how noisome and costly the census had proved, not for myself but for the least among his subjects. He thanked me with his usual courtesy, well beyond that owed to a lowly recordsmith, and bade me return to my usual duties.

But each day since then I have remembered the child, and wondered what his name, the name I would know as I heard it, would prove to be.

About the author:

Francis W. Porretto is an engineer, opinion-editorialist and writer of diverse fiction. He lives in a ramshackle ranch situated in one of the remaining rural parts of Long Island, NY, along with one wife, two stepdaughters, three dogs, five cats, and too many power tools to count. In his spare time, he operates the ETERNITY ROAD website (www.eternityroad.info), a fount of libertarian/conservative/pro-American political and cultural opinion, from which redoubt he rains shafts upon the forces of creeping statism, moral relativism, and political correctness. He's been working for ages on his *Realm Of Essences* series, four fantasy novels whose central motif is that Creation was a subcontract job. Apart from his ability to use "sesquipedalian," "vermiculations," and "anfractuosity" in a single sentence, there's essentially nothing interesting about him. Just ask his wife!

SHORT STORY
SECOND PLACE

SWAN SONG
©2004 by Lenny Willoughby

To say that I love my pet swans is like saying "Oprah likes food". They are my reason for every peaceful morning coffee I've ever had. I love to watch them swim by, acting as if there was nothing in the world more important than the rippled wake their triangular feet make. They glide softly and elegantly with no apparent worry for the events surrounding them.

I awoke Sunday morning—my favorite coffee sipping morning of the week—to a blinding snowstorm. I thought about my significant others and, wanting to check on them, I decided to walk down to the backyard lake. Bleary-eyed, bundled up, snow boots on bare feet and mug in hand, I arrived at the lake's edge to get a shock. Guinevere, my girl, no longer a maiden as of last year, was dead. A lump of hairball-choking proportions formed in my throat, causing me to gasp, coffee streaming forth onto the frozen ground. You see, the pair of Arthur and Guinevere had finally mated this last spring, after a long dry spell. It had taken a monumental four years to produce the heir apparent. Unfortunately, he (the signet) became sushi for the resident snapping turtle this past summer.

But, I digress.

The thing about swans is they mate for life. So, as to be expected, my Arty was quite a ball of wet and lonely down. What to do? A new mate was the only solution, for me as well as Art, because I was already missing Gwenny something un-naturally.

On Wednesday, after the appropriate mourning period for a dead Swan, which is about three days—sort of like it was for my Uncle Pat when Aunt Freda died—I rode 45 miles to visit the "Swan Man Extraordinaire of Ohio," where I purchased for $300 ($200 more than Gwenny the First) a new love for my sad knight, Art, and his lonely Camelot, the backyard lake.

Clive, the "Swan Man Extraordinaire of Ohio," assured me we were not rushing Art, and that all would be well.

Wrong. So very, very wrong.

From the moment I put Gwenny II in the lake, Art chased her, bit her, tried to drown her, and stampeded the ducks after her. One may laugh in incredulity at this point, but the herd was moving toward her in a most unfriendly fashion. Apparently, the three-day mourning period was a mite short for Art. In a way, I thought this rather sweet—for the first two weeks.

Being the helpful matchmaker that I am, I knew it was I who must step forward to help nature take its rightful and timely course. That course and time schedule being mine, naturally. This was a plan riddled with problems from the start. If you will recall, when I began my story I stated how I loved to "watch" nature, i.e. the swans. A Nature Gal—being defined as a person who is involved with or in the act of participating in nature—is not exactly how one might describe me. Having coffee and gazing romantically from the heated backyard Gazebo at my loving pair is about as close to nature as I get.

In fact, I have a garden, but my rule is to never touch dirt. So then, simply put, I don't do dirt and "Swan Hunter" I am not.

What to do? How hard could this be? I simply had to catch the male swan while he was sleeping...or resting...or something, and make him understand that Gwenny II was his new love, and then all would be well. Right? I mean...a full-grown woman (hear me roar) is no match for a bird. Right? Well, let me tell you, when those lovely white bulldozers spread their wings, they reach out a good four feet wide. And they flap. And they excrete. Oh, yeah, they excrete great gobs of indescribable foamy stuff. And, I think they aim it, too.

So, after several big game hunting-like strikes, I decided I needed to enlist my hubby, the dentist-hunter-sailor-runner-all-around-outdoorsman type, to help.

His advice: "Don't! Let nature take its course."

Who was he kidding? I had been knee-deep in swan offal for two weeks and was hopping mad at the situation. Art had knocked me down by hitting me in the chest, as I was feeding him no less, with his very, and I mean *very*, sharp bill. He swung a left hook that planted me square on my bottom with my feet bicycling in the air. My daughter was watching from the top of the hill and commented later that I looked like the Queen of England (while on my back) waving to the crowd that I was okay. (My apologies to Elizabeth II of England; as I am sure she doesn't wave while in a horizontal mode. Or, if she does, it is such a horrific mind picture that I just have to let it die here). Little did my daughter know that my waving, as she called it, was really my throwing out the shelled corn so I would not be attacked while reclining (another horrifying mind picture). But, more than anything else, I was worried about the "swan do" coating my back, as I was beginning to slide down the hill in a rather unpleasant fashion.

Art was not appreciating his new light of love (actually about 45 pounds). And no amount of cajoling was making him seek out his new bought-and-paid-for $300 sexual partner. For heaven's sake, he wouldn't even let her in the water. He would put his head down and stretch out that long neck and swing right at her like a major league ball player.

Never wanting to be outdone by the animal kingdom, I packed up the SUV—my mall assault vehicle—and decided to recon at Gander Mountain, the local sports store.

I knew that the solution lay inside those walls. In actuality, I thought they, the clerks I mean, would be sure to know what I should do to catch this fellow.

Blank stares. That's what I got as I explained my predicament. People shook their heads and looked really sympathetic. Ha! I knew with a sickening certainty born of recognizing that "here is a real Wacko look," I was that evening's dinner conversation topic in many a home.

Thinking I must prevail as a higher up on the food chain, I began to put together my own plan of attack. Walking through the store with "help you" people now avoiding me, I spied a massive net displayed on the middle top portion of the center area of the fishing aisle. It was too large to be put on the floor and displayed vertically. No sperm whale could have had a chance against that baby!

I knew I had found my answer. I mean how hard could it be to sneak down into the backyard lake area with a net on the end of a shiny chrome-colored metal tube large enough to catch Moby Dick and just snag that bird?

I must admit that sneaking up on a swan is a lot easier when it is dead, referring to my experience of that earlier morning. Stalking a live, seventy-five-pound male who is not too happy about a lot of things (even if he has been bought a new $300 date to replace his past love) might prove a bit daunting. Not being a doomsayer or a quitter, I left the store with my NET.

The first problem arose when I realized the net was a little bigger than my 4-wheel drive vehicle. I thought, *Oh well, I can do this. After all, I have squeezed into a size twelve skirt for eons, which should have been put to pasture about 9 years ago.* I further encouraged myself by quietly stating a number of times, "There is no problem here."

I felt my temperature beginning to rise when several men dressed in camouflage on various areas of their bodies walked by snickering. Really, where is the chivalry of years gone by? (Later, my husband explained they were probably afraid. Men will travel in packs like that when they snicker. No self-serving male ever snickers alone.)

After some rich and colorful language, I had the net squeezed into the car between the seats with the large hoop area lying vertically and the butt-end sticking out the back. Knowing that it would be just my luck to be picked up for some minor violation, I tied a red cloth on the end of the net. When I attempted to enter the car, it was evident that it was going to be similar to the tight skirt situation. I was doing it, though...fitting in... come you-know-what or high water. I ended up having to sit partially *in* the net. Yes, that's right: my elbow and half of my body was netted. But, having got it—and myself—in there, believe me, I was not going to adjust anything. I was leaving.

By this time, I had a small audience that I pointedly ignored. I turned out of the parking lot and went about forty yards. A soft orange glow was emanating from the dashboard. The "Check Engine" light was flashing. Of all the luck. But, not to worry, I was only two miles from our local gas station, which I pulled into.

Kenny, our high school fellow who pumps gas, looked in and said, "How can I help you Mrs. Ansel?" I explained that the light had just come on and could he check things? He said not to worry, that the light would hold until the other mechanics came in nearer to the morning time, and I could drive safely home. He never mentioned a word about me sitting in the net or the fact that I could not get out of the car. So, wanting to explain what I was doing, I said, "Hey Kenny, don't you want to know about the net?"

He just looked at me, stepped back from the car and said, "No, no I really don't. Just keep on doing what you're doing Mrs. A. Have a nice day."

Well, I never!

Off I sped. Arriving home, I encountered my next problem. How does one get a whale retrieving net *out* of a car? As the door of the garage proceeded up, the dog, Meka, happily pounced out to greet me. She watched intently as I pulled, pushed, rammed, swore and generally made a jerk of myself retrieving the net. I managed to bonk her on the head several times. After a few short minutes, she retreated to the back room inside the house, surely safer.

Our garage is attached to the houses, so through the door I went to the house entrance. I got the net through the door with little problem and was congratulating myself on my adeptness when I a heard a terrible glass crunching sound and a tiny explosion. I looked up to see that I had taken out two light bulbs with the net and broke them off in the socket. Great! All I could think of was just getting myself around the corner to the back porch and out through the door with no more mishaps. As I turned the corner, Winston Churchill, my African Parrot, whistled his hello. I turned to acknowledge him and hit the hanging kitchen light with the net. This caused the light to swing in a two-foot arc. I swiveled to reach for the light, to steady it, and belted the parrot right off the cage and onto the floor with the butt-end. The dog came running in to the kitchen to see what the screaming was about. The parrot was howling like he was *in* the Amazon, lights were broken and swinging, and I was not even outside yet. My frustration level was growing with a beginning dislike for the Swans. Now, I know this is not the rational way to think about this, but rational had left my mind a long time before batting the bird off the cage.

To get outside the house without hurting, destroying, or maiming anything or anyone else became my primary objective. Little did I know what awaited me outside.

I had been thinking that once I purchased the tools for the capture, upon returning home I would switch to my outdoor clothes. Therefore, my mode of dress was one of a shopper not an outdoors person. However, at this stage, I felt that my choice of apparel was the least of my worries. I needed to get safely outside and try to contain this crazed situation ...and being dressed like either a Neiman Marcus want-to-be or a sheepherder made little difference to the damage occurring around me.

Once through the porch door and in the open, I felt somewhat relieved. Now to the original mission, which by this time almost seemed like it had all started yesterday. Not a low heel in sight, my coat flapping in the breeze, I started my trek down to the lake.

I was beginning to think I was in the clear when I felt my feet getting rather cold. Locating the source of my discomfort, I noticed my $85 pumps were slightly muddy. Upon further inspection, I found the hems of my crème-colored, tailored slacks were also turning a little brown. By the odor wafting up in my direction, I was suspicious that the slacks' brown, uneven border was not *just* a mud problem. Undaunted, I continued with the net in hand, down to the bank of the lake where, to my surprise, I encountered no swans.

I looked to the left and then to the right. I crouched like Hiawatha on the hunt and moved closer and closer to the water. I spied the male, Big Art, sleeping on the lower edge of the bank. Ah, finally it was going my way. My luck had changed. I must also admit to thinking that I would certainly be in fine fettle when the Great White Hunter (my husband) came home to see, in spite of his warnings and total disinterest to the situation, that I had not only persevered, but also successfully righted the course of nature.

In stealth mode, I started. So far, so good. I was only twenty feet from Art when his head went up. He looked a little startled and began to rise. Here is where I got a big surprise. He had always looked big in the water, but on land and this close, he was immense. Instead of running from me like any intelligent animal about to be netted, he charged. As I tried to regain my footing on the incline of the muddy and offal-covered hill, my shoe started to sink in the slop. I pivoted to go up the hill and left my shoe where it stuck in the swan poo! Thinking that the hissing sound was getting very close to my backside, I used the net's shiny metal tube end on the ground to try and lever myself upwards toward the top of the hill. The cheap piece of garbage, that I had so carefully gotten home, started to bend. Where is the justice in this world? My arms starting flapping and whirling like some comic book winged warrior woman, which only succeeded to totally throw me off my already impugned balance. The small squeaking sounds I was making turned into a full roar of indignation as I pictured myself sitting in the middle of the wet smelly bank dressed like a happy afternoon shopper. It was within seconds I knew for certain...I was doomed.

As the bill of the swan connected with my posterior, I, being only human, and trying to save myself by using all available pressure in my body to push forward to escape the immediate danger, did something most mortifyingly natural: I expelled gas.

There was immediate silence from the rear (not mine, I mean where the swan was). I turned to look for my nemesis to stave off the next bite-attack, only to see him standing totally erect and bobbing his head up and down. I thought, *What now? Is he telling me with swan body language, "You are done for?"*

All motion stopped, then he bobbed again, throwing out his wings in a karate kid-type pose. He made little chortling sounds, which then turned into gurgles. He looked a little dazed, rather stricken actually. Then, it hit me. Through a little increased body pressure and function (or dysfunction, one may say) I had solved my problems. Art had found his Gwenny II. It was I. At last, the fellow was in love.

Broken net in hand, one shoe on and one shoe off, muddied, offaled, designer clothes splattered in odiferous splendor, I looked—or sounded like—all that, and a little more to him.

The attack had stopped, but I was now under a new threat. Trying to pick up the pieces of what remained of my dignity, I pulled myself up the hill and back to the house with little incident. As I looked back, a bewildered, love-lorn glance was being passed in my direction by you-know-who. I, however, was so glad to be moving toward safety that I barely felt sorry for the artful swain. (No, that is *not* a misspelling.)

Later that evening, when I had enough courage to relate the entire story to my husband, he listened with the concerned deadpan that let me know he was close to laughing. I had thought better of telling him how I had imagined it all, but I did humble myself enough to tell him about assaulting the swan with my bodily functions.

Most quietly and seriously, he looked at me and said, "Well, Honey, I guess the problem is solved. And, really, it was *your* Swan Song, too."

About the Author:

Lenny Willoughby resides in Warren, Ohio. She is a truly passionate entrepreneur believing that discovery and exploration are gifts meant to be experienced. She has extensively traveled the world, living and working in many different cultures. She has owned and operated different business throughout her lifetime and hopes to do so again.

She writes from her soul and loves it. She has written most of her life, and is currently completing a novel. *"I feel privileged to be alive and experience what life has to offer."*---spoken like a true entrepreneur.

VISITING THE BONE MAN
©2004 by Tish Davidson

We park beyond the ball field, past the dumpsters, and walk back to the Bone Man's yard. The South Carolina sun sifts through the trees where dainty green buds are beginning to unfurl. I shudder as if someone has walked over my grave.

Drugs Is Dangerous, announce two-foot-high shaky letters, complete with crude skull and crossbones, on the Bone Man's weathered shack. From the dog run, a beagle with three pups watches silently, hungrily. Half a dozen squirrels chase each other through a complicated wire enclosure that includes a nest box and small, dying tree. Caged white doves mutter among themselves.

Between the rabbit hutch and the pigsty, behind the turkey pen, and spilling out across the front of the unpainted clapboard house lie heaps of graying bones: jaw bones missing teeth, rib bones, clavicles and scapulas, huge horse-size femurs, and delicate cat-size vertebrae. No one is in sight, but in the driveway a new, red GMC truck sporting a pair of moose antlers on its front bumper overshadows the small home behind it.

The silence presses on us. I feel Helen, a mortified sixth grader, dragging along behind me, holding tight to her little sister's hand and counting the seconds until I will chicken out and we will leave. She senses the fight-or-flight response is about to kick in, and there is more flight than fight in all of us.

Calming my adrenaline surge, I take a deep breath and call, "Hello! Hello, Mr. Bone Man."

No answer.

"Mr. Bone Man? Hello, Mr. Bone Man."

"Mom, shut up," whispers Helen.

Ignoring her, I knock at the side door. No answer.

"Let's go. No one's home," she croaks.

I knock again. Still no answer. Just as Helen's stiff shoulders start to ease, we hear a faint sound inside. The door cracks open about two inches.

"I'm looking for the Bone Man. Someone in Marion sent me."

"Go 'round the front," a dark face mutters into the crack.

After a long, uncomfortable wait, the front door opens. On the threshold stands a tall black man of about sixty wearing a starched white shirt, dark vest, tie, and a red Phillies baseball cap decorated with brown feathers. The Bone Man makes no attempt to come out or to invite us in. He simply stands, waiting.

"I, I, I...we're from New Jersey," I say, as if that excuses my bad manners, my barging uninvited into his life. "I, we, we're looking...looking for something, for people, special people who know about life, people who aren't so locked into the system." Even to myself, I sound like Chatterer the Red Squirrel on speed.

Sucking more air into my lungs, I settle my weight evenly on both feet, and think back to the reasons that explain why we are here.

If you listen to me, I'll tell you that we are here in Nichols, South Carolina, because I am lusting to see lives different from my own. I am fascinated by people whose interpretation of the American dream goes far beyond a house, a car, a job, and 2.3 children, people whose ideas of success don't fit neatly into the little boxes on the census questionnaire.

If you listen to my daughters, I am just wandering through the rubble of my mid-life crisis.

This trip has been five years in the dreaming. It began with school lunches. I loathed packing lunches. Every day my kids ate the same thing: American cheese, white bread, lettuce—no mayonnaise, no mustard, no butter for Helen; plain peanut butter on plain bread for Susan. Day after day, week after week, year after year, those innocuous brown paper sacks that could have held something mysterious and enticing—hummus, falafel, sushi—remained boringly familiar.

I hated those lunches because they mirrored my white-bread life. In our tedious corner of suburbia, discussing who ran late for the soccer car pool passed for analytical conversation. Speculation over whether the public-school principal really was a former nun was good for a week of gossip.

About the time Susan ate her five-hundredth peanut butter sandwich, I started collecting clippings about unusual, off-center people. I found a story about a woman who wove dog hair sweaters made from combings of her dear departed companions, and one about a man who farmed worms in a warehouse in an urban industrial park. I was captivated by a couple who used their life savings to start a center to rehabilitate stranded whales, and by a masseuse who performed deep massage therapy on skiers in the winter and race horses in the summer. This collection of what I called "my Edge People" came to dominate my thoughts. A good day was when I found a new story. A bad day, and there were far too many of them, was when I ended up discussing the pros and cons of blonde highlights with middle-aged women.

My dreams, however, were like children: I lost control over them as they grew, until suddenly I found myself living with obsessions as headstrong and unpredictable as any teenager. Like characters in a soap opera, my Edge People took on lives of their own. I'd abruptly cut off my Thursday morning coffee companions' speculation on whether the "right people" could jump the swim club waiting list to bore them with stories about my people on the fringe.

My husband and I analyzed their theoretical economic prospects. My kids speculated about their kids. To me these people represented something lacking in my own community, that same admirable combination of determination, non-conformity, and faith in the future that had propelled my Mennonite ancestors from Switzerland to Pennsylvania in 1710.

Above all, my Edgies were living proof that you can escape your school lunches. So, after years of talk, it came to seem perfectly reasonable to leave my husband behind in New Jersey, take my children out of school, and set off on a five-month trip around the edges of America to find out what was missing in my comfortable suburban life.

Now, face to face with the first person I have encountered who was a true non-conformist, I was the one on edge. Looking nervously up at the Bone Man, I began again, explaining that a man at the Laundromat in nearby Marion had told us about the Bone Man's unusual healing powers and suggested we come to visit him.

"You got any family 'round here?" the Bone Man asks.

"No. I'm just passing through, traveling with my children, trying to show them something of their country and to learn something about the people in it."

At the mention of children, the Bone Man perks up.

"Those the only two you have?" he asks.

"Just these. Helen is twelve. Susan is seven."

I drag the reluctant kids into view. He looks at them hard, as if making up his mind about something.

"That big one," he says, "she has a beauteous head of hair. Don't let her cut it."

Still standing on the doorstep, the Bone Man talks about his skills. "I was born psychic, able to read palms, read signs, read minds. It's a gift from God. I'm from a line of healers three hundred, four hundred years old. I learned healing from my great-grandfather and my grandfather. The healing comes from Jamaica. No, I wasn't born there. I was born in New York. This was my granddaddy's place. Been here fifty-five years."

The Bone Man stands erect and speaks so softly that I have to crowd him to hear. After a few minutes, whether he is tired of me standing six inches from his chest or simply has decided we are harmless, he surprises me by saying, "Come on in."

As the door opens, I see a boy about thirteen with Rasta braids slip out the side entrance. The small room is oppressively hot and smells cloyingly of herbs. In one corner, a kerosene heater burns with an open flame. The uneven wooden floor is crowded with a maze of shabby, dark, overstuffed furniture. Several acrylic portraits of children, elaborately framed and out of place in the rundown house, hang on the walls.

A table shrine dominates the right side of the room. "This here's my great-grandfather and my great-grandmother," says the Bone Man. Behind me, Helen recoils as if she expects to see mummies rise up off the table. With a sharp intake of breath, she pivots and is almost out the door before she realizes he is talking about two wooden statues flanking the shrine. The figures, one male, one female, look African to me, but when I ask him where they come from, he answers, "Jamaica." His collective memory as a healer, passed on as oral history from teacher to student, does not extend beyond the Caribbean.

Three wooden logs, about two-and-a-half feet long and four inches in diameter, lie on the table between the figures. Each log is decorated with carvings and feathers, inlaid with small glittery stones; "Diamonds" the Bone Man calls them. A white dove wing, an assortment of ivory bones, and a plastic statue of the Virgin Mary draped with a rabbit's foot complete the tableau.

Handing me one of the logs he says, "This here's a healing stick. It's over three hundred years old. It's passed along from healer to healer. I got it from my grandfather." He offers Susan and Helen the rabbit's foot. Susan, who has been gaping at the shrine, examines it with interest, caressing each toe. Helen gives me a withering look and backs away, refusing to touch it. Blood, bones, and other animal parts play an integral part in the Bone Man's work, and some of the caged animals in the yard seem likely to become a part of his ritual healing.

I try to pin him down on exactly what kinds of healing he does.

"All kinds," he answers vaguely. "Gangrene, I can heal that if I gets it soon enough. And heart trouble. I gets lots of calls for heart trouble, ohhh yes." I never learn whether he means lovesickness or the physical ailment.

"Do people ever ask you to do evil things with your powers?" I ask, wondering how much I dare question him.

"Oh, yes, but I don't. There's always them that wants revenge. Men can do enough evil on their own. I works for good. I counsels, gives advice. You saw my sign out there, drugs is dangerous. Kids these days have lots of problems." He pulls an ID card out of his pocket. "I'm a parole officer. I help place kids in new homes and all like that. It's hard for them. I tries to counsel them."

He picks up a necklace of small bones that look like rat vertebrae from the table shrine and passes it to Susan. "I makes these for my parole kids. They can wear them to school. It helps them make friends and takes all the evil mischief out of them." Gently, the Bone Man reclaims the necklace and lays it back on the shrine.

The smell of herbs and the heat leave me feeling queasy, so I suggest we move outside to look at the bones in the yard. Some of the piles are three feet high.

"I love bones," the old man says. "I've gone hunting for dinosaur bones with university men. There's bones I've helped find in universities all over the country. I take my son down to Georgia with me hunting bones and herbs. He's my youngest, twelve, same age as your daughter. I'm teaching him to be the next healer so he can take over after I'm gone."

I ask him about his other children.

"My daughter, I bought her a trailer right across the road so's I could be near my grandchildren. I've got a son who's an artist. He painted those pictures of my grandchildren inside. I've got another son. He's an M.D. Right before he graduated medical school, he took me over to the university and let me look at slides he made from a thousand-year-old bone in my collection. It was wonderful. Like looking back into the past."

The Bone Man sighs as if looking back far beyond his own life. He is still a mystery to me, but he no longer frightens me. Here is a man working in the system as a parole officer, sending his son to the University of South Carolina Medical School. Here is a man who believes that blood and bones and herbs and faith will heal the body and change behavior. Somehow the Bone Man has successfully reconciled these two cultures within himself.

As we leave, the Bone Man touches Helen's head and mutters, "beauteous hair, beauteous hair. Is she an actress?"

Helen keeps moving, eager to get away, but I halt and turn to face him. Helen, with her bountiful black hair and pale freckled skin, works professionally out of New York on commercials, small films, and television programs.

"Thought so," the Bone Man says complacently, leaving me wondering about those psychic powers that are a gift from God.

About the author:

Tish Davidson has written for magazines and newspapers about topics affecting parents and children since 1989. Her most recent books for middle school readers are *School Conflict* and *Prejudice* (Franklin Watts/Scholastic Library Publishers, 2003) and *Competition* (2005). She has an advanced degree in biology and also writes medical articles for encyclopedias and textbooks. Tish lives with her family in Fremont, California. She and her daughter Susan are volunteer puppy raisers for Guide Dogs for the Blind. "The Bone Man" is a true story that occurred in 1993 during a five-month trip around the edges of the United States with her daughters.

THE SENSITIVE GUY
©2001 by Edith Thornton

Timothy Crutch had never been a ladies' man. A few pivotal incidents stuck out in his mind as reasons for his failures, but like many problems, his ran deeper than a couple of misfortunate episodes. Nevertheless, he persisted in blaming his bad luck with reputations. As a young child, he was known as the "the boy who ate ants." His father told him they would build an army in his intestines, so he'd only done it once for a neighborhood audience, but the incident was seared in the minds of his peers. Girls thought he had cooties and that surely a boy who ate ants also ate his boogers.

He was only able to trade in his status as gross and peculiar when he cried during a history class viewing of *Gone With the Wind*. While Melanie slipped away on the 30-inch screen, Timothy wept, so moved he was that the world should lose her. His classmates, most of whom were not one bit emotionally engaged in or paying attention to the film, found Timothy quite entertaining. They tittered and heckled. When the teacher turned on the lights at the end of the movie, Timothy continued to weep. After all, how could Rhett leave Scarlett?

From that moment on, Timothy Crutch became Mr. Sensitive, companion to women everywhere. Girls wanted to be with him, tell him their problems, and wet his shoulder when their *real* boyfriends hurt them. It didn't take long for him to realize that this new attention from females wasn't the kind that would get him in their beds. Oh no, these girls just wanted to talk, to be friends, to stick up for him when tough boys called him a wuss, a flamer, and a girly ass.

Now that his school days were behind him, he found himself a thirty-two-year-old virgin. Being a nice guy was so tiresome, he was ready to do something drastic.

In the last few months, his masturbation rate had gone up to five times per day. The slightest thing set him off: a TV commercial with girls in bikinis, a model on a billboard, the striking woman who cut his hair. He wouldn't settle for just any woman though. Oddly enough, each year he didn't have a girlfriend, his standards went up rather than down. He had built up sex and the ultimate woman in his mind for so long that possibly no one could fulfill his dreams. It wasn't necessarily that he hadn't had a few opportunities to have sex. There was the woman with bad teeth who smelled of menthol cigarettes who had offered him her love, and the overweight Yoga instructor who had invited him to her house to "show him a few moves." He knew he'd turned his back on plenty of chances. He admitted he was a little timid about intimacy, especially since he'd waited so long for it. But he had to have his standards, didn't he? Maybe something had to give, but the idea of changing his life was a vague notion for which he had no concrete plans. He had terrible anxiety and knew that given the proper moment he would do what was necessary. It wasn't long until Rebecca presented him with the opportunity.

Rebecca was Timothy's oldest and dearest friend. She knew all about his sexual frustrations and insecurities. She too had a bit of trouble with the opposite sex. Her narrowly defined political views often got her into heated arguments with the men she went out with. She would often lament, "All I want is a man who believes in the same things I believe in. Is that too much to ask?" Apparently it was. However, at least she dated, whereas Timothy was rarely able to interest a girl past the first meeting.

Rebecca had invited him to a demonstration for women's rights. She often asked him to join her at these events with the hope of setting him up with someone. Each time he would end up with yet another friend. He had so many girl companions that he was on the phone almost constantly. They would sucker him into going shopping with them, and an entourage of chatty women would lead him through stores. He was their token male; there to get them safely to their cars at night, nothing more. The thought of meeting another girl who just wanted to be friends sickened him. So, he declined Rebecca's offer.

She showed up at his doorstep anyway, carrying a purse the size of a suitcase; her hair bobbed in two pigtail braids. "Aren't you ready yet? This is sooooo important. I do this every year, and it is most invigorating," she said. She handed him her bag and leaned over to hike her black tights up to their proper place at her waist. He drooled as her skirt rode up. Rebecca had laid down the law years ago that she wasn't interested in him "like that." Today he was feeling brave. He wanted to say things he'd never said, even make her mad.

"Can't we stay here and get naked?"

"What's wrong with you?" She looked at him like he'd eaten ants. "Hurry up, I left the car on."

Whenever he tried to move a relationship with a woman to the next level, she would look at him like he was about to commit incest. Some of his female friends thought he was cute in a sad, pitiable way. Many were convinced that he was a closet gay. One such girl had said, "Oh, honey, you don't like me. Society has pressured you into thinking that, but a crush on a male is perfectly normal, and much more your style." He had such a boyish face, a weak, squeaky voice, and a skinny frame. He looked half his age easily, like he hadn't even hit puberty. Women just couldn't imagine him as anything other than an asexual teddy bear. Harmless, comfortable, trustworthy, Timothy Crutch. When he said something like, *Let's get naked*, it appeared so out of character from his looks that it was incomprehensible. His sensitive guy reputation very much owned him rather than the other way around.

Inside Tim a fury was growing, a stifled rage that had been building since his childhood, an anger that would no longer be silenced.

At the demonstration, women were trying to take back the night. Rebecca had driven them to a college campus where a few hundred people stood in an open brickyard holding candles and listening to testimonies of violated women. A stage had been set up at the front of the crowd, complete with a podium and microphone. The current woman in the spotlight spoke with the edge of a knife in her voice. At the appropriate times, Rebecca chanted loudly beside him, "Take back the night!" The November air was chilly, and Timothy's nose ran. He sniffled but was not alone. Others were sniveling around him—though out of sadness, and many were crying outright.

Their tears confused him. The woman speaker seemed to him to be empowered with a strength he had only dreamt of. These were survivors—weak creatures who had seen the dark side and come out of it more alive than they'd gone in. Their voices embodied freedom and vitality, a chance to start anew. He could taste their joy and his; the tether had been cut and the unraveling of someone locked away had begun, someone who was pissed off, who'd been abused, and who wasn't going to take it anymore. An ephemeral peace came over him, and he felt the strongest affinity with these battered women than he'd felt with anyone else in the entire human race.

He spotted an interesting young woman in the crowd wearing a blue scarf around her neck, three heads to his left. She had short, ebony hair that contrasted nicely with her alabaster skin. She was the sort of woman who wouldn't give him the time of day—the kind that might catch him staring and retaliate with a sour visage. In that one look, he would be scolded, told she was out of his league and always would be. He would be reminded of the hierarchy and his classification as an unattractive person—a nerd, who might never be happy in his whole miserable life.

Beside him Rebecca was rocking on the toes of her Mary Janes and rubbing her gloved hands together. He swept her up, bag and all, in a fierce hug. Then with more determination than anyone would have thought possible, Timothy Crutch marched into the heart of the crowd.

"Where are you going?" Rebecca asked his retreating figure. He could not answer her, because he was going somewhere he had never been before.

Only moments later, he leapt the steps of the stage as if he were a great athlete. He walked to the podium with such deliberation that the violated woman naturally stepped aside. In the voice of a trained politician, he spoke clearly and with purpose into the mike, "I, TIMOTHY CRUTCH, WAS RAPED."

He proceeded to weave the most fictitious tale he had ever told. "Brutally, I was kidnapped and sexually assaulted by my own father." The captivated crowd murmured what sounded like the Amen's of churchgoers. "In my youth, my manhood was taken. Violently, I was stripped of all dignity." He made eye contact with the woman in the blue scarf. Was he speaking for her benefit, and maybe only to her? It felt as though she were the driving force, moving him forward in this outlandish story.

Yes, it was all technically a lie, yet the words he spoke had a certain truth behind them, he thought. He *had* been raped, goddamnit. Wasn't it a good way to describe his life? The longer he spoke, the more he became convinced. "I declare to you; I was raped!" His checks blew in and out of his face as though he were filled with the air of an accordion. "The strong prey on the weak, but I won't take it anymore!" His assertions made him high, like a runner in his tenth mile. "We must fight back! Together we can beat this and reclaim our lives!" He heard clapping and encouragement, and it bolstered his confidence and his own belief in a vision he was creating as he went along. For the first time in his life, Timothy Crutch was being cheered instead of jeered. He was a survivor.

"I want to thank my friend Rebecca for accompanying me here

tonight and leading me towards recovery." As he mentioned Rebecca's name, he was seized with an unanticipated panic, as if he'd forgotten where his extemporaneous speech was going or been asked a question for which he didn't have an answer. "Uh..." He rubbed his eyes and looked blankly into their trusting faces. "Thank you," he managed to say. He ended his great story to thunderous applause. Surely these were sounds meant for a hero, he thought. He didn't want to leave the stage, so he bowed grandly. Tucking his hands behind his back, he leaned over as far as flexibility would allow, like a pianist to a standing ovation. He continued in this manner, because he had a strange premonition that when it was over the wonderful feeling of intrepidness would disappear; it would be a dream from which he would awake largely disappointed.

"Tim," someone whispered below him. It was Rebecca. He was still leaning over, as if waiting to be knighted, and he could see her hair braids caught under her huge pocketbook. Her eyes were those of a true friend, and they tried to warn him of impending embarrassment. He got the hint and exited the stage a revitalized and energized new man, ready to continue the re-creation of his life through storytelling. Climbing Everest, skydiving, making his first million, he could invent it all. He could be anyone he wanted to be.

After the rally, Rebecca was waiting for him. It turned out that she didn't buy a word of "that bunch of malarkey," as she described it. "I've known you for seven years. You tell me everything. You couldn't keep a secret like that if your life depended on it."

"I could so," Timothy argued. He feverishly persisted in defending his story of violation mostly because of Eloise, the woman in the blue scarf. She was quite moved by what he had overcome. His admission had given her the courage to come forward and share her own heartbreaking testimony. In gratitude, she wanted to take him out for dinner. The last thing he needed was Rebecca spoiling his fun. Anyway, how dare she question him?

Weren't close friends supposed to trust and support one another? Some friend she was, he thought.

To his recollection, and he *would* remember, Timothy had never been asked to dinner by a woman. Eloise had looked at him with such admiration that he had felt powerful and calm in her presence. He had a past now, and though he couldn't have known this would make him more attractive to her—especially such a strange and in many ways embarrassing backdrop for a relationship, he did feel that she liked him, maybe even loved him. How could she when she hardly knew him? He wasn't sure, but he believed it was happening.

It wasn't only Eloise who loved him; two of his "just friends," Gwen and Vicky, thought his revelation made perfect sense. It was the key to why he was such a sensitive guy. With a little explanation and motivation behind his effeminate characteristics, he became less asexual and somehow almost handsome. Surprisingly, Rebecca was the only person giving him a hard time—the only one able to see through him. In a small way, he found this disappointing. In a much larger way, he found it quite exciting. It meant he could truly change his life and become whomever he wanted, limited only by his imagination.

On their date, Eloise wore a royal blue dress with a white scarf. She reminded him of a peacock, tall and rare. They dined at a nice Indian restaurant with wall pictures of elephants and couples engaged in *Kama Sutra*. He hadn't much experience with Indian food, so he let her order for him. Later this proved to be a mistake, because spicy didn't even come close to describing his dish. The dinner conversation, to Tim's dismay, revolved solely around him and the "incident," as she referred to it. She was as inquisitive as a reporter, and all his attempts to change the subject were thwarted.

"Is your father still living?" she asked. Her voice had the melodic innocence of a child, unaware of forbidden topics.

"My father?" Tim, momentarily confused, repeated like a parrot.

"You said your father was the one who abused you. Did you not?" she asked again, in what Tim felt was a voice too loud for the small restaurant. An image of his elderly father, now retired, who had worked for thirty hard years as a cook in a steakhouse and who had encouraged Timothy to major in computer engineering in college—a career which had been more than generous to both of them—made Tim feel like the biggest *schmuck*. His father would be horrified, absolutely mortified, not to mention disappointed, if wind of this ever came his way.

"He's dead," Tim replied. He hoped this answer would make her less curious.

"I thought so. I think it would be hard to come forward with your story if he were still alive." She took his answer as a license to talk more in-depth about his feelings toward his father, his father's death, and what Tim was feeling since his testimony the week before. She fired question after question. As the entire lower part of Tim's face burned from the food, he answered with lie after lie. He thought maybe the further he got from the truth the less interested she would be, but she was enthralled. She was attracted by what she saw as his modesty. Each lie came forth as a kind of confession. On a roll, Tim decided that his career as a computer engineer was too boring, so he embellished it a bit.

"I made my first million on the patent for the CD-ROM," he explained.

Later at a pastry shop, over dessert and coffee, he wanted to seem more experienced with women. So, he told her that Rebecca was his ex-girlfriend. The evening was long, and in the end, he had a monster story the details of which he could hardly remember, but he really *needed* to know them. Once already she'd nearly caught him. She wanted to know his therapist's last name (she needed one herself), and he couldn't even remember what he'd said his therapist's *first* name was. He told her he'd call her with the information. When the date ended, she kissed him goodnight and made plans to see him again. She had a wonderful evening, she'd said.

Timothy was determined that this time things were going to be different. Eloise was sexually attracted to him; he could feel it. Keeping up with his made-up life had exhausted him; nevertheless, he couldn't help but believe that the dishonesty was worth it. He could never fool Rebecca of course, but everyone else was all too happy to be convinced. A woman like Eloise would've never talked to him in a million years if he hadn't jumped on that stage and told his story. She embodied all the women who had ever rejected him, all the girls who wanted to be "just friends," and every dream he'd had of a woman in the last thirty-two years. He was never giving her up. If he had to bamboozle his way into the next millennium, he planned to stick to his story—if he could remember what it was. Eloise was quick. He knew he couldn't afford to be careless again. He opened his desk drawer and pulled out a pad of paper and a pen. Okay, now how had his story started?

About the Author:

Edith Thornton holds a BA from North Carolina State University in English Writing and Editing and is currently a graduate student at Fordham University pursuing a Masters in Teaching English. Residing in Long Island, Edith teaches at a local high school. "The Sensitive Guy" is her third short story to be published. Her first was "The Race" in Carolina Woman magazine and her second, "American Gothic Romance" published in Moxie magazine.

GRACE SUCCUMBS TO PRESSURE
©2001 by Ritch Brinkley

Food was not easy to come by in the Spring of 1932 in Middle Tennessee, as a young man's fancy was more likely to turn to thoughts of hog jowl and Hoppin' John than love. Entertainment wasn't even on the list of necessities. So, when the first block ad announcing

Grippo, The Human Fly

appeared in the *Rutherford County Courier*, the citizens of Murfreesboro began to buzz like bees in a hive.

From the first plain advertisement stating Grippo's upcoming visit to scale the three-story Rutherford County Courthouse, speculation ran wild as to who—or what—Grippo might be: a circus act, a World War I flying ace, a Kentucky daredevil, a practical joke. One rumor even asserted that Grippo was the ghost of local Confederate hero General Beauregard T. Cuthbertson.

From Groundhog Day through Easter, the simple box ads appeared weekly on the page charting the progress of livestock prices:

Hogs: up two cents
Poultry: down a penny
Grippo: scheduled for Easter Sunday

With clock-like precision every Monday morning, a plain manila envelope would be found under the *Courier's* front door. The contents were always the same: a crisp one-dollar bill (the cost of one week's ad) and explicit instructions on how and where the ad should appear.

Ordinarily, Easter marked a preoccupation with entries for the new Rhododendron Queen, always crowned four weeks later at the annual Mayday picnic in Shiloh Park. And, with approximately the same predictability, golden-tressed Rose McPherson, sole daughter of Angus McPherson (McPherson-Sweeney Mercantile) would claim the honor.

In fact, the only mystery regarding sweet-faced Rosy was why no local gent had been able to coax a marital promise from her puckish lips.

But that speculation paled in comparison to the frenzied gossip revolving the enigmatic human fly's visitation as Easter morning finally came. The gullywhumper that more than quenched the thirsty crops on Saturday night had not yet ceased as the first eager folk arrived on the courthouse square for Grippo's seven o'clock appearance. An assortment of hand-polished motor cars, beat-up pickups, jitneys, well-worn buckboards, and backfiring tractors crowded the spacious square around the august edifice as woven picnic hampers containing southern fried chicken and honey-filled scratch biscuits were passed from hand to hand, along with freshly squeezed lemonade.

Just as the town clock struck a resounding seven chimes, a pudgy, freckle-faced towhead screamed, "There he is! It's Grippo!"

A cacophony of excited voices verified the deliberate approach from between the red brick buildings of a slender figure clad from head to foot in a peculiar ill-fitting jersey costume of mottled green, gray, cobalt, and pale yellow. Two cornflower blue eyes peeked out of narrow slits in a bizarre head mask at the buzzing but well-behaved assemblage of farmers, field hands, merchants, and their families.

Now the Rutherford County Courthouse wasn't Kilimanjaro, but the granite cupola atop the third story—where births and deaths were recorded—was round, perfectly smooth, and the object of intense local pride.

As the oddly clothed figure reached the stately old building, Grippo began to ascend the south wall, creeping hand-over-hand, making slow but steady progress up to the second floor, then on to the third. The conical and domed cupola fairly glistened in the recently ended light rain as the spellbound crowd watched Grippo begin to slither up its sloping face.

Applause erupted from the excited spectators amidst shouts of "Bravo!" and "Go Grippo!" and shrill whistles came from adolescent lips as the daredevil moved up the cupola.

Then, less than nine feet from the top, Grippo suddenly slid down the dome and fell the three stories in a matter of seconds. The loud, viscous thump silenced the sickened onlookers as his body slammed onto a concrete walkway. Not even the tiniest movement could be perceived as the first fleet lad reached the lifeless body sprawled face down across the sidewalk. A tearful field hand gently rolled Grippo over and delicately slid the mask off the crushed, bloodstained face. A wave of nausea swept through the crowd as a hysterical feminine voice screamed, "That's Cletus Ward!"

It was an unnecessary revelation, inasmuch as everyone for miles around knew the shy, stammering young editor of the *Rutherford Courier*. His editorial expertise was almost as well-known as his many unsuccessful attempts to convince the virginal Rhododendron Queen to reciprocate his oft-professed undying love and manly worthiness.

There would be no further attempts to establish the hapless Grippo's bravado as his slender frame lay in state for all the county inhabitants to file by and pay their last respects.

As details of the extraordinary attempt by the extraordinarily ordinary man gained momentum, he approached legendary status. A local bluegrass band even spun the tragic tale into an oft-requested song, replacing the words of the ancient Scottish ballad known as "McPherson's Lament."

After years of earnest but feckless pursuit, Cletus had

apparently been pushed into one final grandiose effort to convince the fair Rose of both his courage and ardor. He was seemingly propelled into desperate action as the sought-after Rose's legendary beauty began to attract swarthier, well-heeled lads from far and wide. It would only be a matter of time before Rose's father began to exert pressure to supply him with a grandson and heir to take over his share of the mercantile.

Apparently, every week from Groundhog Day through Easter, Cletus had carefully placed the simple envelopes containing both payment and explicit instructions for where and when the ad should appear, his identity well hidden in the frequent pre-dawn Stones River fog. Most of the time, Cletus himself opened the message as the small newspaper staff looked on with growing curiosity.

Each spring as Easter dawned in the center of the Volunteer State, an enormous bouquet of bell-shaped, fragrant rhododendron blooms mysteriously appeared atop Cletus Ward's simple grave in Rutherford County Cemetery. Rumor has it that they were placed there by the aging spinster daughter of Angus McPherson, whose beauty began to rapidly fade after that rainy dawn in the Great Depression year of 1932.

And the annual floral tribute proved once and for all that Grippo's near perfect ascension succeeded in its intended purpose—at least in the heart of one Rhododendron Queen, whose reign had finally ended.

About the author:

Ritch Brinkley spent his entire life as a professional actor on stage, screen, and television, from 1969 through 1999. Upon retiring from "showbiz", Ritch taught acting for the camera at The University of Wisconsin-Stevens Point before moving to Florida's Emeral Coast, where he writes a biweekly movie column entitled, "Before the Lens" for the *Beachcomber*, an entertainment tabloid. He wrote and performed the one-act monodrama "Hemingway: In Earnest", and holds a BS in Communications from the University of Texas at Austin, and an MFA in Acting from Florida State University. He is best remembered for the decade he spent on television's *Murphy Brown* as the lovestruck cameraman "Carl". *Grace Succumbs to Pressure* is loosely based on an actual incident he learned about while touring the theatres of Tennessee, Virginia, and North Carolina in the early 70s.

4 PIVOTAL MOMENTS IN THE LIFE OF A GOURMAND

©2001 by Alicia Davis

Four months ago
Margarita's Restaurant and Bar
Chicken Fingers and French Fries
Those present: myself, boyfriend, another couple

"Alicia...are you ok?" A look of concern crosses my boyfriend's face as he notices my unusual pallor and vacant expression.

"I think I need to go to the bathroom for a minute...I'll be fine." But I'm lying, and not for the first time, because I can already feel the telltale tightness building in my stomach and can vaguely hear the gurgling in my lower intestine. This is not a good sign. The other couple is staring at me over their margaritas.

"You sure?" he holds back my chair and I stand up, not too straight, because my cramping bowel doesn't allow much more than a ninety-degree angle.

"Yeah, I'll be right back."

Three seconds later and I was back all right, unable to negotiate the steps and having broken out into a cold sweat, embarrassed and totally convinced I looked like a junkie strung out on crack.

"I have to go now...now, I have to go..." I mumble, sweating profusely, pale and sounding like Dr. Seuss in my delirium. Great first impression. My boyfriend hands me the keys and I stumble out of the restaurant, ready to toss my spicy chicken fingers and fries in the direction of the first person I see in the parking lot. So much for a nice dinner out.

"Whatever you do, don't eat the fish!" I rasp at some girls, who quickly shuffle away from my hunchbacked, sweaty self. I might have even drooled.

I guess you could say that total physical and social humiliation stirs the perverse in me. Even at my worst, I can't help a little self-effacing humor.

Damn chicken.

Throughout my entire life, my stomach and I have enjoyed a tenuous relationship at best, built upon a foundation of mutual respect and loathing. I've discovered through years of clinical trials and rigorous scientific testing that as long as I heed some basic tenets, we get along fine. But even in the most solid of relationships, my stomach and I tend to test our boundaries every now and again.

HYPOTHETICAL CONVERSATION BETWEEN ME, MY STOMACH, AND MY INTESTINE:

Me: God, I would kill for a Dairy Queen Blizzard.

Stomach: Righhhht. Don't even think about it.

Me: I haven't had any cheese or milk today; I bet I could get away with it.

Stomach: How quickly we forget that Dannon yogurt this morning.

Me: I'll have an Oreo Blizzard, please.

Stomach: I'll make you beg.

(Ten Minutes Later)

Me: Oh that was so good, I think I'm ok.

Stomach: Ah, the magic words...Intestine, do your worst.

Intestine: *Rumble rumble grrr grrr...*

Me: Ughhhh, I'm going to die! I'll never eat another Blizzard, I swear it!

Stomach: *Ha ha ha ha*! (Maniacal laughter).

This scene has re-enacted itself thousands of times throughout my intestinally challenged lifetime. Restaurants, lunchrooms, banquets, movies, you name it. There isn't a bathroom in the tri-county radius that I haven't sat in, clutching my stomach, vowing to find religion at any cost. I've discovered that my fickle stomach isn't Catholic, Buddhist, Methodist, or Presbyterian by any means.

And, when my stomach does its weekly re-creation of the battle scene from "Braveheart," I often regress to the mentality of a five-year-old. Just this weekend I envisioned checking myself into the hospital, getting pumped with all kinds of drugs, and calling my boss to tell her I'm in the emergency room in Virginia with a bad case of the runs. And I want my mom.

My mom, herself a sufferer of a torturous stomach, is often the only person that comforts me in my darkest hours. Not that she physically pats my shoulder and feeds me chicken soup; no, that's definitely not her style. Hers is more of a psychic comfort. Because no matter how bad off I may be, she always has a story to top mine, and she has absolutely no qualms about telling me how stupid I am.

Me: Mom, I'm sick.
Mom: Well, what did you eat?
Me: Nothing, just some Dinty Moore Beef Stew.
Mom: What, are you crazy?
Me: I know, I know!
Mom: I guess you will be on the pot for a couple of hours. I was up at three last night with diarrhea.
Me: Mom! I don't want to hear that!
Mom: Why not? I'm your future. Get used to it, kid.
Me: *Click.*

Thus began my painful indoctrination to the world of intestinal fortitude. These lessons haven't been easy, as any unwilling student can attest. But the truth hurts.

And so does Dinty Moore.

LESSON 1: COLESLAW
February 1990
Harbor Restaurant, Florida
Coleslaw Appetizer
Those present: myself, roommate, two friends

"This place is beautiful!" I stared in amazement as we stepped off of the boat onto the fresh wood of the dock. The Harbor Restaurant was cedar and paint with a myriad of glass windows, located on the water's edge. They even had their own launch so boats could pull right up to the establishment after tooling around the Florida waters for a couple of hours. Very chic.

"Do they valet park?" My roommate Marie joked as she, too, stepped off of the swaying speedboat. Her immaculately kept hair was somewhat awry from the riotous ride we had enjoyed on the way over.

"Sometimes," came a male voice from the back of the boat. It was Mark, the owner of the boat and somewhat of a braggart. I overlooked the shortcoming as he was graciously allowing us to use his place on an impromptu jaunt to Florida during a hellacious snowstorm up north.

He tied the boat up with a casual deftness and hopped over the side to stroll up the main walk. "Come on," he gestured. "You'll love this place."

The Harbor Restaurant was as imposing on the inside as it was on the outside. Fashionably dressed patrons chatted over long-stemmed wineglasses and plates of Brie and strawberries. Marie and I felt conspicuous in our wind-blown hair and comfortable shorts as we followed Mark to a table conveniently located in the center of the large dining room.

"Isn't this great?" he effused, turning to regard the wine list with aplomb. I was silent, thanking my wisdom in choosing to forgo the keg party T-shirt and opt for a more conservative look.

Marie hadn't been so lucky: her short shirt barely covered the lines of her bikini that she was trying desperately to hide.

"Yeah, great," she mumbled without much enthusiasm.

To my disappointment, the menu was filled with succulent fare like roast duck and veal tenderloins. All I wanted was some chicken, plain and breaded, not filleted or sautéed or flambéed. My general rule of thumb: if I can't pronounce it, I probably can't digest it.

Thanks to the understanding waiter, I succeeded in ordering chicken fingers from the kids' menu and breathed a huge sigh of relief.

"Hey, does anyone want my coleslaw?" Marie asked, addressing the table. Something about the smell of it offended her delicate nose.

"I'll take it," I volunteered, reaching for the small glass bowl. Coleslaw was a personal favorite of mine from childhood. I remembered my grandmother making gallons of it for family picnics and the slightly tart combination of carrots, mayonnaise, and greens made it irresistible. What I loved best, though, was the crunchy sound it made when I bit into a mouthful. That juicy crunch told you it was freshly made and ready for consumption.

I made short work of the coleslaw, noting its excellent taste and texture. "That was great," I said. For some reason, it came out sounding more like "phlat wuth glate." Marie looked at me with a funny expression on her face.

"What did you say?"

I looked at her, puzzled. "Ith glate." I frowned myself. Something felt wrong, I thought.

Marie began to nudge me. "Alicia, I think you should go to the ladies room, something's wrong with your lips, they look funny."

I had begun to notice a burning sensation growing on my lips. That coupled with an extreme itching in the back of my throat became almost unbearable. I pushed back my chair and made a hasty exit to the restroom, careful to shield my mouth from the other patrons, afraid they'd see my enormous lips growing out of control and start pointing and staring and throwing cutlery.

I sped into the posh ladies room and practically pushed aside a woman to look in the large oval mirror. Sure enough, my lips had doubled from their normal size and were stinging like crazy. I looked like a cosmetic surgery gone awry. "Damn the coleslaw," I muttered, coming out as "damb the coll thlaw." Other women in the ladies room shied away as I began splashing my face with cold water in a futile attempt to shrink my lips. Worse, I was having trouble swallowing, as my throat seemed to shrink.

After a few minutes of sub-zero dousing, my lips halted their forward progress and seemed content to blister. I looked up from the porcelain sink to see a well-dressed woman staring at me in horror.

"Collagen," I explained with a shrug. I watched in amusement as she hauled ass out of the bathroom as fast as her Gucci heels could carry her.

Damn coleslaw.

LESSON 2: CORN
July 1993
Berwyn, Pennsylvania
Corn on the Cob and Hot Dog
Those present: myself, family, summer boyfriend

"Hey Alicia, Jim's on the phone. He's coming by in an hour or so," my mom called out over the deck, cordless in her hand.

"Thanks!" I flipped another hot dog on the grill, the scent of the grilling meat co-mingling with the summer breeze and the fragrant sycamore next door.

My stepfather yelled up from the kitchen. "Do you want any corn on the cob? I have a couple of ears here."

"Yeah, I'll be right down. I'm just finishing up the hotdogs."

Summer in the Verguldi household meant cookouts. My stepfather's first major acquisition after buying the house was a grill. The roof needed to be fixed and the windows had gaps the size of picket fences, but we had a grill. So as my stepfather embarked on a quest to become a master griller, so every single-family gathering was hosted at our home, much to the chagrin of my mother, the master dishwasher.

"So, Jim's coming over?" my little sister Nicole asked, a paper plate with a hotdog roll on it in her hand. For a young girl, she has always had a precocious interest in my boyfriends.

"Yeah, a little later," I replied absently, wielding tongs as I picked up a well-done dog.

"Are you going out?" she pushed. Always the questions with her!

"Why do you want to know?" I pushed back, handing her the hotdog and nudging her on her way.

"Will you play a game with us?" And there it was, the crux of the matter. I smiled as I grabbed a hotdog of my own and headed downstairs to join the rest of the family.

"After we eat. Hey, the corn looks good!" I piped up, grabbing an ear from the ceramic dish on the table outside. What a perfect summer afternoon, I thought, settling down on a plastic lounge chair as the sound of Jimmy Buffett echoed from the Bose speakers out over the backyard. My aunt and her brood had arrived, bearing devilled eggs and potato chips.

I was a little nervous about Jim coming over, even though he had met my parents. We'd been dating just a month or so, but he was good looking—probably the best-looking guy I had ever dated—and I couldn't wait for my snooty aunt to get a look at him.

I turned my attention back to the corn on the cob I'd just procured and smothered it with butter. Corn on the cob was always one of my favorites. As a child, I would help my mother peel back the husk and pick out the individual hairs that would inevitably stick between the kernels, before throwing it into a big pot. And nothing could compare with biting into a sweet mouthful, the butter dribbling down my chin and the shells sticking between my teeth. It was heaven and a perfect reminder of a summer afternoon.

I had devoured one piece when my stepfather held out another.

"Want the last one?"

I felt my stomach tighten up slightly and knew I had reached my limit. I prided myself on getting to know my stomach better after many years of gastronomical torture. "No thanks, I'm kinda full."

I'd better go lay down a little bit, I thought, feeling my stomach gurgle slightly. I didn't want to be bloated when Jim came over. I made my way into the basement and lay down on the couch, unbuttoning my jean shorts in order to comfortably expand. Looking at my watch, I figured I had about a half hour before Jim arrived, enough time to make a trip to the bathroom and still look gracious.

Screw gracious, I thought fiercely not five minutes later, inching myself off the couch onto the cold cement of the unfinished basement. If there is a Hell, I've found it, I told myself as I wiped away the sweat off my brow. What seemed like contractions ripped through my abdomen and left me curled up in a fetal position on the cold floor, my sister and mother alternately staring and laughing at my pitiful state. "This isn't funny," I snarled, pulling up my knees as I felt prepared to birth a watermelon or something unimaginably large.

"Alicia?" A soft masculine voice called down from the top of the stairs. My mother and sister looked up and I closed my eyes in mortal embarrassment.

"Hi Jim," I gritted out as my bowels threatened to play "Wind beneath My Wings" for the umpteenth time. Oh please, don't let me fart in front of him, I beg my stomach.

"How about a hot dog?" I ask as nonchalantly as possible. I know he is horrified; I don't even have to look.

Damn corn.

LESSON 3: HAMBURGERS
October 1991
Western Steer Steakhouse, Patuxent River, Md
Hamburger and French Fries
Present: myself, Tara

"Feel like going out to dinner?" Tara casually asked me one afternoon following class. I stopped walking and looked at her. Tara and I were never that close. We'd been in the same circle of friends, lived on the same hall, but definitely not tight.

"I guess so, where?" I was skeptical but willing to make an effort if she was.

"How about the Western Steer up on 235?"

It certainly sounded better than what the cafeteria had planned for our nightly torture. As freshman, we were spoiled by our parents' cooking and came to college to experience a rude awakening in the culinary department.

"Sure, come knock on my door when you want to go."

We parted ways and I left for my room pleasantly surprised. Tara was a hit with the upperclassmen, pretty and thin and gregarious but cursed with what I considered a huge nose. She was a rich girl with horses in her stable at home and a closet full of trendy clothes. Why she suddenly wanted to hang out with me I had no idea, but the steakhouse on 235 held appeal.

The car ride was filled with chatter as we drove up the scenic highway. "How was the Door last night?" she asked absently. "Was Tom there?"

Ah, now we're getting somewhere, I thought to myself. "No, I didn't see him." Tara had a crush on the guy I was secretly hanging out with. Not secret enough, I guess.

The conversation turned to the lacrosse team as we pulled into the restaurant and were seated at a table by the window.

I carefully perused the menu, trying to decide between a thick cut of steak and a succulent burger. I was always a sucker for BK's flame-broiled double cheeseburger, and the picture on the laminated menu held promise.

"What are you getting?" Tara asked without looking up.

"I think I'm going with the burger." I announced, closing the menu with a snap.

"Steak sandwich," she added, picking up her soda and swirling the straw.

We made small talk until our food arrived, discussing the upperclassmen she'd met, the girls on our hall, and the screaming peacocks that have made the campus their home. Before long, the burger was placed reverently before me, a mound of meat barely contained by a thick, round roll and heaped with tomatoes and lettuce and bacon. I silently praised Southern Maryland cooking and bit into a meaty mouthful.

Forty-five minutes later, we paid the bill and shuffled out the door like two overstuffed pigs.

"I'm not feeling so good," Tara muttered as we ambled back to the car.

"Your stomach?" I asked sympathetically. I knew what that was like.

"Yeah, it's sore."

We got into the car and pulled out of the parking lot. I looked at her face in the light and saw sweat beading on her brow.

"Unbutton your pants and expand your stomach with air, you'll feel better." I was a veteran of bad stomachs and knew just what to do.

Tara did it and smiled a little, "Hey, you're right."

But as her symptoms eased mildly, I felt my own troubles just begin.

I proceeded to loosen the fastening of my own pants, careful not to let too much of my distended abdomen peak out. "I think I'm feeling a little sick, too."

Tara eyed me as we stopped at the red light by the video store. I mentally calculated that I had a good ten minutes before I was in real trouble, and prayed to the stomach deity that we'd make it back in time.

The red lights seemed to stretch out for an eternity as far as the eye could see, and when a slow-moving Cadillac pulled out in front of us on the windy one-lane road, I suddenly knew that I wasn't going to make it.

"I'm gonna be sick," Tara moaned, clutching her stomach as I made a frantic grab for the wheel. My own stomach did a round-off double handspring as we pulled into the drive heading back to campus.

"God, I hope there's a parking space out back," I whimpered. Prince George, our dorm, was notorious for its lack of parking. The closest lot, affectionately nicknamed "Guam" for its lack of proximity, was a good three minutes away.

"Maybe we could park out front and leave the flashers on," I offered, seeing no spots available.

"They'll ticket me!" Tara wailed. "Could you park for me? I'm gonna throw up."

I thought about my own dubious odds of getting back to the dorm in one piece, but she was right, the car would sit there for a good hour at least before we'd even be able to rouse ourselves from the toilet. She would definitely be ticketed. I had to suck it up.

"Ok, I'll drop you off here and bring your keys by."

Tara gave me the most profound look of gratitude and ran from the car, hunched over. If the upper-class hotties could only see her now!

No surprise, Guam was where I ended up. I managed to get across the street and through the first lot when an excruciating spasm hit me full force. I continued on behind Caroline, the dorm adjacent to ours, bent over at the waist and sweating at least five pounds off my body. I'm not going to make it, I thought dramatically, clutching my stomach and falling onto the damp grass beside a tree. At least that felt cooler.

If only my mother could see me now, I thought, lying behind the tree. She'd give me the biggest "I told you so" lecture of all time. She gave up burgers years ago.

I knew I couldn't just lie there, so I began crawling like a commando soldier across the lawn, careful to avoid open windows. I made it all the way to the edge of the grass and, in an act of sheer willpower, dragged myself to my feet and ran for the side door. I prayed that the bathroom on that hall was unoccupied since I'd never make it to the third floor.

Another freshman that I'd seen in my history class stood at the sink brushing her teeth. Seeing my wet and haggard state, she almost dropped her toothbrush.

"What happened to you?" She whispered, foam still on her lips, making her look rabid.

"The peacocks," I explained, "They chased me from my car...better look out!"

She grabbed her toothbrush and ran out without rinsing, terror in her eyes.

Damn burger.

LESSON 4: DAIRY PRODUCTS
November 1992
Golden Corral Restaurant, Patuxent River, Maryland
New England Clam Chowder, Macaroni & Cheese, Ice Cream
Those present: myself, college boyfriend

"Hey, what do you say we hit the Golden Corral before we head to my parent's house?" Tom threw out as we packed for the weekend. He knew I was nervous. Although I had met his parents once before, we were actually staying overnight this time. That was a much bigger deal.

"Yeah," I said with a smile, "That'd be great."

The Golden Corral is the Maryland equivalent of Old Country Buffet. Patrons grab a tray, order their meat from the counter, then mill about the buffet tables picking up whatever items catches their fancy: chicken, coleslaw, mashed potatoes, mac-and-cheese, and rolls. Tom and I were big fans of the "Corral" as we called it, and ate there at least once every month or so in order to escape cafeteria food. (I had refused to go back to the Western Steer.)

"What are you getting?" Tom whispered to me in line. My eyes were focused on the menu printed above the main counter, my forehead creased in serious concentration. This was important stuff: the steak or the chicken?

"I'm thinking the chopped steak." I finally announced, trying to ignore Tom's bemused look. I always got the same thing, but I liked to make a show of trying to decide and he knew it.

"Good call."

Three minutes later we wound our way through the maze of patrons and tables and picked out our side dishes.

"Roll, macaroni looks good, some mashed potatoes, ooh...New England Clam Chowder." I eyed the bowl jealously. Now, I knew that I had a slight dairy problem, but

I'd been pretty good lately. I'll only take a small cup, I thought, ladling the thick, creamy soup. But definitely no ice cream, I told myself in a stern voice.

"Let's get some ice cream for the road," Tom suggested with enthusiasm. For a guy who was rail-thin, he sure could pack it in.

"Uh, I don't know, I'm kind of stuffed," I demurred, but Tom was already at the dessert table, filling up a bowl with soft-serve vanilla ice cream, my favorite. What could I do? I grabbed a bowl and dug in.

"How are you feeling?" Tom asked on our way out to the parking lot. We'd been dating long enough that he had been the unwilling recipient of my stomach's machinations more than once.

I smiled at him over the hood of the car. "I'm fine, let's get going."

A half hour later, Tom pulled over about midway to our destination. "Let's stop for a video." At that point, I wasn't too sure that was a good idea. I had unbuttoned my pants after the first ten minutes into the trip. My stomach was playing a symphony and I just wanted to get where we had to go as soon as possible.

"Tom, I'm not feeling very good, why don't you run in and pick something out."

He looked at my pasty face and agreed. Relieved, I proceed to let out the nastiest, smelliest gas explosion ever in the history of the Western world. I immediately felt better, except for the almost unbearable smell that lingered in the car. Frantic—and now thinking clearly—I rolled down the windows and opened the door, trying to wave the offending air away as fast as possible.

I got in a good minute or two before Tom came back, jumping in the car. "I got the ..." He stopped dead and his face scrunched up. I looked as innocent as possible under the circumstances and offered a timid smile. Being the gentleman that he was, he didn't say a word.

"Never mind," he continued and turned over the ignition.

Some twenty minutes later, we pulled into the winding driveway of his immaculate house. In my agony, I barely appreciated the sheer size of the place. "I've got to use your bathroom," I yelled out, forgetting my bag in my haste and running for the front steps. Tom let me in and pointed me to the direction of the nearest bathroom, which I sped to without even an introduction or a "Hi! How ya doin?"

Once settled and having emptied my abused stomach of its contents, I noticed the perfectly arranged hand towels on the rack and the exquisite cleanliness of the entire bathroom. I felt like such an idiot. What would his parents think?

After five minutes, I emerged from the bathroom, drained and feeling a little better. I barely made my hellos when I ran back for another ten minutes. At that point, I feel better acquainted with Tom's toilet than with Tom's parents. That's not a good thing.

Thinking the worst was behind me, I freshened up in front of the mirror. I wiped my sweaty face and tried to rearrange my hair. I wanted to look somewhat civilized, not like some street person they let come in and use their can. I wondered if I should leave five bucks on the table for their trouble, or at least to cover the cost of the toilet paper I'd used. I walked out into the dining room to Tom and his parents, who were chatting with one another. All three stopped and looked at me. I was about to offer a sheepish apology and thanks when Tom's mother started to laugh.

"Whaddya got, the shits?"

I was so mortified that nothing came out of my mouth. For the first time, my humor failed me and thus my humiliation was complete. Wait until I tell my mother about this one, I thought.

Damn clam chowder.

About the author:

Alicia began dabbling with the written word at age 12, when she started penning episodes of G.I. Joe for the amusement of her friends. She expanded her repertoire to include mushy love poetry and romance novels until a self-effacing and sarcastic style appeared in her mid-twenties, which she enthusiastically embraced as her true voice. In 2001, Alicia earned a master's degree in English & Publishing from Rosemont College and is currently the Director of Public Relations at a private school in Villanova, Pa., until she can afford to quit her day job.

THE SOUTHERN-MOST GHOST
©2005 by J.E. Moore

Saturday morning, July the fourth

It was hot—damn hot. The relentless heat, coupled with a few other noxious irritants, had made our home in south Florida a very uncomfortable place to be at the moment. Definitely not Chamber of Commerce weather—it never was during the summer.

I was reading aloud from the newspaper and commenting about various tidbits in the weather section. "Geez, the forecasts are so bad it's almost like reading the A section." Something interesting caught my eye. "Ah, ha! Joyce (my wife), you know that brown halo we've been seeing around the sun?"

"Yesss...it's ugly. What about it?"

"You're not gonna believe this. It's African dust."

"What?"

"Yep, African dust. Somewhere around eight hundred billion zillion tons of dust from the African deserts have drifted across the Atlantic Ocean and stopped right over the south Florida mainland."

"That's all we need, but I question your numbers."

"Yeah, whatever. But not only that, the easterly winds from the Gulf of Mexico are holding it in place, and because of the drought, there's no rain to dissipate it."

"Great. Is that why my eyes are tearing, my nostrils burn and the air stinks?" she complained.

"No, that's from the everglades fires—over twenty thousand

acres burned so far."

"Why doesn't someone put them out?" she asked.

"Too many and too far away—can't get firefighting equipment to them. We're at the mercy of Mother Nature...and the pyromaniacs."

"You know my breathing isn't that good. I'm not a jogger like you. I'm suffocating. When am I going to get some relief?"

"Don't know. Looks like we're in for the long haul...unless..." I flashed a smile, "It's time to get outta Dodge City!"

We loaded up the SUV and headed south to Key West, below the smog bank. I had read there was a small, low-key, five-kilometer road race on Sunday morning. But then, every activity in Key West was as *low* as you could get—so low it made the heralded, laid-back California lifestyle look like a Chinese fire drill. For starters, there seemed to be a dire shortage of non-tourists. You couldn't find a home-grown Key West native or actual resident, who called themselves *conchs*, anywhere other than those working in the novelty shops and after their gig was up they'd disappear like a puff of smoke, as if they had never existed. And another strange thing, no one walked the virtually crime-free streets outside the established tourist section: Mallory Square. There were nothing but vacant streets on the whole island, Why do you suppose that was? I had remarked several times before that Key West was the island of the phantom resident.

Soon, after passing Homestead, Fla, we merged into the usual endless stream of cars, campers and towed motorboats trekking down the only route heading south—good old US1. The scenery was postcard beautiful and the two and a half hours passed quickly. As we crested the Seven Mile bridge, sixty-five feet above the azure gulf, I asked, "Where you wanna stay? Got any ideas?"

"How about one of those nice motels downtown?" she answered.

"On Duval street? I think there's only one left and it could be rather pricey."

"Perhaps not, it's the summer...however, you didn't give me time to call."

"Sorry 'bout that. We'll see what goes." 'We'll see' was my stock answer—it covered everything from the Bubonic plague to the Immaculate Conception.

"A hundred dollars a night! Per person?" My mouth was hanging open. "It's usually half that price. Less!" I argued.

"It's the holiday weekend," the pretty, young receptionist returned defensively. "It's the same everywhere, sir."

"I think not!" and stormed out. "Gouging, outright gouging! That's what it is. I'm not paying that kind of money." I ranted on, "I'm a working man..."

"Enough, John!" interrupting me. "The girl's right, it'll be the same everywhere. Besides, we should have called."

More pain. I crossed my arms and commenced to defuse. Finally, I said, "Let's stop and think about this. There must be *somewhere*." I searched my memory banks and out of the mists came, "Las Palmas Motel!"

"Where?" knitting her brow.

"You remember, we stayed there a few years ago."

"Vaguely. Was that the cheap one on the other side of the island...the deserted part...five years ago?" She shook her head. "All those buildings and roads—no people. There?" with a shrill.

"Hey, *I* saw some people, I think...in the daytime. Humm... I'm not sure now. But so what? Let's go check it out. Nothing to lose, right?"

We hopped in the car. Joyce said, "I don't remember where it was."

"I do," feeling better already. "It's just one block on this side of the southern-most point in the United States. Remember the marker?"

"Yes...it's a huge block of concrete shaped like a bell and painted like a deep-sea buoy."

"Atta girl! Right where US1 dead ends." I was impressed she

remembered the particulars. "And how about the guy who looked like a bum, the one who tried to sell us the conch shells?" I added.

"Yes, and the old Cuban fisherman who came over and told us not to buy them. He said the shells had been drilled and the conchs inside had been pulled out alive. He said they were cursed because the conch souls had been ripped from their home and would never be at peace."

I laughed, "That bum was really pissed that the fisherman warned us off, wasn't he? Amazing, some of the weird things we remember isn't it? Cursed souls...zombie conch meat. Yummie! Think of that next time you chow down on one of those greasy fritters."

Las Palmas looked just the same: a square consisting of twenty units enclosing a botanical garden and a strip of ten much older units on the far side of the parking lot.

Inside the manager's office, "Carlos, you're still here? You look well," extending my hand and receiving his handshake.

"*Si*, thank you, *señor*. It's been a while since I see you. *Como esta? Y Senora?*" to Joyce. She nodded, "Hello" in return.

"*Bien*, Carlos, *bien*," in my limited Spanish. "And Yolanda?"

"Good," he beamed, pleased that I remembered his wife's name.

The pleasantries aside, I asked, "So how about a room, *amigo*? Just one night this time. Cold beer, boiled shrimp, a run in the morning then back to the frozen northland," I spoofed.

"Ah, sorry, no room." Dead panned—he was not joking, "All filled up."

"What?" I scanned the smoldering parking lot from the office window: no cars—not one.

"Convention in town," he explained.

"Convention of what? Vampires? There's no cars. Did they fly in as bats?"

"Vampires, bats? I think, no." He appeared pensive, as if he were mulling the idea over. Finally, he said, "Everyone went to the high school auditorium. Mel Fisher, the deep-sea salvager, he make a new sunken treasure display today. Grand opening, first day, national news!" he raised his palms outward, "And the holiday weekend..."

"I told you we should have called..."

I glared at Joyce. "That horse is dead, thank you very much."

I turned my attention back to Carlos, "Would you happen to know of another place we might find a room? Something we can afford? The motels on Duval Street want blood or body parts."

He stared at the countertop, "No, sorry, *señor*."

"Boy, this is turning into a real crock." I pressed, "Come on, *amigo*. Are you sure you don't have one? To be cleaned? Refurbished? We're not picky."

He glanced up and looked across the lot at units one through 10. I spied a single key still left hanging behind him. It was marked #8. "How about number eight? Is it empty?"

He twitched as if he'd been pinched on the arse. "Eight? Oh. Empty? Er, yes, it's empty."

"Well! How about it, Carlos?" I challenged. "Old friends here."

"We no rent that unit. We save it for emergency."

"An emergency!" I barked. Was I being insulted? "In case the President drops by? Got news for you, he ain't coming." I was more than a little peeved by then. "So, is it clean, or what?" I didn't wait for the answer. "We're *not* driving back to Miami. We'l take it."

Yolanda was carrying room supplies and watching us from the courtyard. She waved to Joyce then stopped dead in her tracks when she saw her husband reach for the key. Her hand went to her mouth. She dropped her basket—a dozen little bars and plastic bottles scattered across the cobble stoned walkway. She closed her eyes and made the sign of the cross.

Carlos reluctantly removed the key from its hook. Placing it gingerly on the counter, "You look at room first, *si*?

Reaching for my wallet, "I said we'd take it."

"No!" his hand moved to cover the key. "Look first."

"Ok, Carlos. Whatever." I snatched up the disputed key. "Come on, Joyce. Let's go 'look'." As we left, I mumbled, "Be back shortly," while giving him the you-are-wasting-my-time scowl.

Irritated, I quick-stepped it across the burning asphalt, then paused, waiting for her to catch up. "Sorry. I believe my patience is running a bit low right now."

"It's all right, John. Let's get this done and get settled in. I'm hot and getting tired."

"Right," I agreed. "Number eight, we are here. Prepare to be boarded!" As I slid the key in the lock I noticed that the air conditioner wasn't running, and hadn't been for a while (there was no condensation drip puddle below it like the other multiple units on either side. "Just great. It's gonna be hot as a pistol in there."

Being brilliant and analytical, I declared, "We'll turn on the AC then go sight-seeing. It'll be okay when we return."

The door, with a little push from me, creaked open. I flicked on the light switch as we stepped in. It was cold. Not cool. *Cold.* "What the...? How...?" A few more steps. "Geez, it must be fifty degrees in here!"

Joyce shivered. "*Brrr...* it's freezing!" as she rubbed her bare arms.

"I doubt that," being technical, "maybe sixty. It's probably just the shock of coming in from such intense heat." Neither of us bought that. It felt different from just being cold. It felt like a tomb: dank, soundless, no circulation.

"I have goose bumps already," said Joyce.

"Yeah, I can believe it." As we shuffled to the center of the room the hairs on my arms rose. "Static electricity. Must be a new carpet." It was old and worn thin. "Kinda dark. Ah, well, you know, these low budget operations and their forty-watt bulbs...always trying to save a buck." I went to the picture window and drew back the heavy, insulated drapes.

The sunlight revealed the typical motel room of yesteryear: a single double bed, a dresser at its foot, a nightstand in between and a closet-sized bathroom with a small vanity before its entrance.

"Still not too bright in here, is it?" The sun was striking directly on the glass—we should have needed sunglasses except for the fact that the light seemed to die a few feet in. Snuffed out. "Must be smoked glass," I reasoned. It was clear. Joyce pulled her arms across her chest, her eyes darted about the room. "I'll turn on the vanity lamps."

Pop! The single bulb, in a row of four, flashed dead. "Humph! Figures. I'll tell Carlos to get some decent..." as I turned back to her. She hadn't moved an inch—a pillar of stone—except for the eyes: large, straining to see into every corner and crevice. She couldn't.

"You okay?"

No answer.

What was that? Did I detect a slight movement on the ceiling? A passing? I glanced at the outside lot. Nothing. I knew Joyce saw it, too.

"Probably a lizard. I'll tell Carlos to shoo it out."

I stared hard at a corner where I was certain the critter had to be hiding, but I sure wasn't about to brush my hand against the wall to find out. Hell, it could have been a scorpion! Hard as I tried, I couldn't penetrate the darkened haze.

"The light's playing tricks," I whispered, trying not to disturb the unknown. The shadows deepened. It was as if we were developing tunnel vision.

The mirror slowly turned opaque as if a breeze of hot air had whisked across it. A trickle of water formed like a stream of teardrops. Suddenly, a faint noise crept through the room. Very faint, but very clear. It wasn't music. It sounded like a high-pitched wail from far away. I cocked my head to hear better while keeping my eyes glued to the mirror, half expecting to see a face materialize like in a horror movie.

I then sensed an unseen presence nearby. Someone was watching us, very closely. I felt like I was breathing in a vacuum. I took deeper and deeper breaths without fulfillment. The wailing became louder. The hairs on the back of my neck stood up. The presence was all around us—at arm's length. Now behind, now above!

"Oh, God..."

"John! John! It's a *ghost!*" Joyce screeched. "Someone must have *died* here!"

I nearly jumped out of my skin. "Wha...? Who?" I stammered. Joyce bolted for the door, ripped it open, and dashed into the parking lot. I was right on her heels. "How...how do you know that?"

"I *know.*"

I believed her.

She headed for the office but then took a sharp turn toward our car. "I'm out of here! I'm not staying in this town another instant. Don't say an f'ing word, John," she added as I caught up. "I'm going home. Stay if you want."

We talked a few minutes and she calmed down a bit. "Okay, we'll go, but I have to turn in this key first," waving it to emphasize my point. Leading her slowly, my arm around her shoulder, "Just stand over here in the shade under this palm tree. It's too hot to wait in the car. I'll only be a minute. Okay?"

Silently, she simmered, but stood stoic in her assigned place, her back to Unit 8.

Yes, sir, gotta turn in this puppy and find out what spooked Joyce, I said to myself as I hustled toward the office.

I leaned on the counter, tossed the key down, and gave Carols a long, hard look. He appeared rather uncomfortable. "So, no vampires. Just ghosts, eh, *amigo*?" I could see he knew exactly what I was talking about.

He didn't try to deny it. Too much. "Er, ghosts?"

"Yeah, ghosts. It scared the poopy outta my wife."

"Is she okay?"

"More or less. What's the story, Carlos? Did someone actually die in 8 like Joyce thinks?"

He fidgeted for a moment, seeking relief in the courtyard, only to find Yolanda scowling back at him. He mumbled, "Ghost bad for business..."

"Well?" as I drummed my fingers.

"You see her?"

"Her?"

"*Si*. The lady. The lady killed in that room."

"No, thank goodness, but we sure as hell *felt* her...or something...a presence of some sort." I checked Joyce. She was still standing under the palm, a lot calmer looking. Carlos had said *killed*, not *died*, so I decided to risk staying a couple of extra minutes to ask the burning question. "What happened?"

"About a year ago, close to today, her husband kill her. He use his fishing knife. Very messy."

I gasped. "Good God, why?"

"He *loco*...crazy," pointing to his own head. "They come here for several years. He always act like macho man. Loud and pushy. He think he own his wife, no respect. Down deep, I think he act this way because he very jealous person. Jealous of his pretty wife. She *muy bonita*, he *mucho* ugly.

"Anyway, on that day, he come back from fishing with his amigos. Drinking buddies only, they never catch the fish. He drunk." Carlos furrowed his brow. "I think he drunk most of the time." Continuing, "He see his wife hug another man in the doorway of Number 8. He hide behind palm tree, same one your wife standing under. Then, man leave, he run inside, and do the bad thing."

"Gosh, how terrible."

"Worse. Man was her brother, in Navy, just docked at the Key West Naval Station. She no see him in years. He visit...nothing to it. Just a good-bye hug. Her husband never meet her brother."

Flustered, I exclaimed, "Why didn't she tell him right away, when he came in? To stop him?"

"He no listen. *Loco* drunk. Police say he stab her in the throat. No can talk...or scream. Then he gut her like a fish. And do other things too horrible to say," as he gestured toward the lower part of his body. He paused and sighed. "I clean up. Much blood. Yolanda no go in there now, says it is haunted. I think maybe is true."

I felt queasy, light-headed. I thought I was going to barf my lunch. I gave my thanks, but now regretting that I had asked that particular way. Half-dazed, I fumbled my way out.

As we eased out of the lot, I saw that the door was closed and the drapes were drawn tight again. "Sonnabitch..." I knew damn well no one had entered after us. Joyce's were riveted straight ahead and she asked no questions.

I bade farewell to the Southern-most ghost, an anguished spirit trapped in her own personal hell: room number 8 in the Las Palmas Motel, Key West, Florida.

We sped away. Never to return.

ATS

(A True Story)

About the author:

J.E. Moore (John) lives with his wife of eighteen years, Joyce, in Davie, south Florida. During the last five years he has written numerous short stories and two unpolished novels. As to date, he is eagerly anticipating his eminent retirement from BellSouth Tel. Co. as an Electronic Technician and plans, forthwith, to tie-up his writings' loose ends. And then, to press forward to new frontiers, "Warp speed! Engage!"

STAR SISTER
©2004 by Karen Konoval

I'm sitting in the parking lot of the Las Vegas International Airport with Jack and Marjorie, a sixty-ish couple from Oklahoma. We're perched on our suitcases, waiting for the shuttle bus to Laughlin, Nevada. The three of us huddle together like grumpy birds on a wire, breathing deeply of bus fumes and checking our watches. There's a bench to our right with enough room for all of us, but a woman in a black chiffon evening gown is sitting at one end of it, picking invisible bits of fluff from the air, putting them in her mouth, swilling them around like mouthwash and spitting them out again.

"What's she doing?" whispers Jack. "Eating bugs?"

"*Shh,*" says Marjorie. "She's crazy, that's all."

The woman spreads her arms like wings and flaps them gently, her sleeves billowing.

"Maybe it's Tai Chi," says Jack.

"*Shh,*" says Marjorie. Her suitcase tips precariously as she leans forward to rummage in her purse. She pulls out a carefully folded stack of tissues, a tin of breath mints, a miniature sewing kit and a cellophaned package of cookies. "Peak Frean?" she offers. "I saved them from the plane."

We sit munching our cookies. The woman on the bench has begun humming to herself. It sounds less like humming, more like a dog testing its vocal chords before howling at the moon.

"I think she's singing now," whispers Jack.

"*Shh,*" says Marjorie. She picks cookie crumbs from her husband's lap into a tissue, folds the tissue into a tiny square and snaps it back into her purse.

"Well!" says Jack. "That hits the spot, doesn't it? Marge? When did we last eat?"

"Four-thirty yesterday afternoon," says Marjorie. "Those wiener biscuit things." She shudders. "And *don't* talk about the shrimp cocktail, Jack. Don't even mention it."

"I won't." Jack grins at me. "How'd you like Vegas?"

"Oh, it was fine," I lie. Thinking back on my evening it's a tired blur of escalators and ringing slot machines, losing my way in one labyrinth after another. "How was your night?"

"Rotten," says Marjorie.

Jack looks hurt. "Aw, c'mon Marge. You were just upset because of that plane business." He turns to me. "I got the...you know."

"Strip search!" says Marjorie, incensed.

"It wasn't a strip search, Marge. But I had to take my shoes off. And I had a hole in my sock. Marge just hates it when I wear socks with holes in them."

"Hmph," says Marjorie.

"But anyway, I guess we had a pretty good time last night, hey, Marge?"

"Hmph," she says again.

"What did you do?"

"Well!" Jack claps his hands. "We were hoping to see one of those shows..."

"*Girly* shows," sniffs Marjorie.

"We're just checking in when this pretty lady comes up and says, do we want to see one for free? Well for goodness sakes, that's better than..."

"Jack likes to get stuff for free," interjects Marjorie.

"Who doesn't? All we have to do is take this free tour, and we think..."

"*You* think."

"*I* think, what the hey! A free tour *and* a free show! So..."

"He signs us up." Marjorie rolls her eyes. "Next thing, we're on a bus going God knows where..."

"Great way to see the sights," says Jack.

"Some time-share condo thing, but we never *see* the condos, we just get stuck in this room..."

"It was a really nice room," he offers.

"...looking at *pictures* of condos and listening to some man blather on. Then when we didn't want to *buy* one of the condos..."

"They were really nice condos."

"Well, sure they were!" snaps Marjorie. "But we don't want one! Anyway, when we wouldn't *sign up* for one..."

"More *information* about one," clarifies Jack. "I would've, but Marge stuck her heels in."

"Because we don't want one, Jack! I'm not going to lie!"

"We might've got our show tickets quicker," he murmurs.

"Sure we would, but that'd be a fib and that's not right and you know it."

"Oh well!" Jack shrugs. "By the time we got back it was six-thirty and our show tickets were for five o'clock."

"We would've had to stay another night just so Jack could see his free girly show."

"I like girlies." Jack tickles his wife's elbow. "Like you."

"Hmph," says Marjorie. She resettles herself on her suitcase, straightening her skirt. "Then we walked downtown. That was Jack's idea too. Somebody told him the slots were looser and there was a free laser show."

"And the free shrimp cocktail," Jack reminds her.

"JACK! *I told you not to mention it.*" She turns to me. "Jack heard that some place had the best shrimp cocktail for free. We went all over Kingdom Come looking for it, but we never found it. Well, we *found* one, but it certainly wasn't free."

Jack leans in. "It had something in it," he whispers. "Something with *feet*."

"*JACK!!*"

Marjorie looks sick. Jack makes a motion with his fingers of zipping his lips and throwing away the key. The woman in black suddenly hops up onto the bench, squatting on her haunches. She bares her teeth and growls.

"Oh...oh my." Marjorie seems on the verge of tears. Jack pats her knee. Another tour bus rumbles past, choking us in its fumes. After a few moments all three of us check our watches.

"You know, it's funny," says Marjorie softly. "I always wanted to see Las Vegas, but I thought...I don't know. I always thought Las Vegas would be those little motels with swimming pools and palm trees, and beautiful show rooms with red velvet booths, and there would be Frank Sinatra singing, or Dean Martin, or Sammy Davis..." She stops, at a loss. "Something with...some kind of magic. You know?"

"Yes," I say, surprised. That's exactly what seems to be missing, what I always hoped to find, too.

"They're all dead," says Jack.

Marjorie sighs. "Sometimes, I guess," she says, "the places you can travel to in your mind are better than if you actually go there."

As if on cue the woman in black lets out a terrific wail. We jump. She's standing on the bench, her arms raised to the heavens, a beatific expression on her face as she howls at the sky. People stop to watch. I see a pair of ladies approaching us. They cut a wide circle around the howling woman, scrabbling over the parking blocks.

"IS THIS WHERE WE GET THE BUS TO LAUGHLIN?" one yells.

We nod yes.

"LENORE! THIS A'WAY!"

A third woman approaches, wrestling with a luggage cart. It's piled high with suitcases in matching sets: mint green, baby pink, and blue with yellow daisies.

"IS SHE GONNA KEEP THAT UP?" yells the first woman. Again, as if on cue, the howling woman closes her mouth and is silent. She looks around, lost; then abruptly steps down from the bench and disappears into the parkade behind us.

"Whew!" says the first woman. "I thought that was never gonna quit."

Marjorie takes her fingers out of her ears. Jack stands up.

"I'm Jack," he says. "This is Marjorie."

"Nice to meet you! My name's Genevieve, this here's Delia and this here's Lenore. We're in from Dallas," she beams. We shake hands, introducing ourselves. All three ladies are dolled up to the nines, wearing crisp dresses and high-heeled shoes, impeccable hair-dos and lots of jewelry. A heady cloud of perfume drifts about them, flowery and sweet.

"Y'all gonna do some gambling?" asks Genevieve.

"Maybe a little," says Jack, glancing at Marjorie.

"Well, we sure plan to!" Genevieve chortles. "Delia here says she heard a voice, says she's gonna hit the motherlode in Laughlin!"

"I sure did," Delia chortles too. "That is exactly what I did hear."

"Are you sisters?" I ask. All three ladies burst out laughing.

"Sisters?" says Genevieve. "Well, I guess you could say so, I guess you just could. You probably won't believe this, but no fooling, we were all born on exactly the *same day*!"

"Really?"

"So, I guess you could call us Star Sisters since we were born under the very same star!"

"Yes," I say.

"At least, that's what our husbands call us. The Star Sisters. That's what they call us, don't they Delia?"

"Star Sisters, that's right," agrees Delia. Lenore nods, giggling.

"We're just taking our semi bi-annual girls' week to howl," explains Genevieve. "Leave the ball an' chains at home, get the hell outa Dodge and have *fun* for a change!"

Marjorie's face is frozen in a polite mask. A wiry man approaches us.

"You folks for Laughlin?" he asks. We nod. "I'm Tim," he says.

"We're right over here."

Jack and Marjorie and I grab our suitcases, Lenore scrabbles with the luggage cart, and Genevieve and Delia set off in the lead with Tim, their high heels clipping over the pavement. They climb into the van first, snagging the front seats. Marjorie heads for the rear seat, pointedly beckoning Jack and me to follow. Jack and Lenore and I help Tim load the luggage. I realize now that the ladies have coordinated their outfits to match their suitcases: the baby pink set belonging to Genevieve in her baby pink dress, the mint green ensemble to Delia who wears emerald silk, and the blue suitcases with yellow daisies are probably Lenore's. While they don't quite match her navy skirt and white blouse printed with cartoon Minnie Mouses, there's something suitably childlike about the big yellow daisies.

Jack dutifully follows Marjorie into the rear seat. I hop into the middle one. Lenore, after failing to squeeze in with her Star Sisters in the front seat—all three ladies are substantially endowed—climbs in beside me.

"Whee—ha!" hoots Genevieve. "Ladies, we're on the fun bus now!"

We all laugh, glad to be on our way. Even Marjorie cracks a smile. Tim tells us that we're going to see some amazing sights on our journey today. We'll travel over the high plateau of the desert and drop down more than three thousand feet to Laughlin and the Colorado River.

"I didn't realize there was an altitude change," says Genevieve. "You bring any of those Sinutabs, Lenore?"

"I dunno. Let me look." Lenore opens her purse and stares into it. "Nope. But I got some Juicy Fruit."

"Give her some of that," says Delia. "Gimme a stick too."

Lenore digs out the Juicy Fruit. Genevieve offers it around. By the time the package gets back to Lenore, it's empty. I offer her mine.

"That's okay," says Lenore. "I got good ears."

As we start out across the wide, eerie plain of the desert, Tim points out the joshua trees and the yucca plants, commenting how hardy they are to survive in this unforgiving land with no water, growing a scant quarter- or half-inch a year.

"Don't it rain at all?" asks Delia.

"Oh, sure it does," nods Tim. "And when it does, it comes so fast the flash floods'll fill this plain like a basin, so sudden you don't even know it's happening, you couldn't even open your car door."

"No kidding," says Genevieve. She and Delia scooch in closer to each other. Lenore hugs her purse to her chest. Jack stares blandly out the window. Marjorie and I crane to watch the traffic on the road ahead. There seems to be a lot of it, going at a frightening clip.

"What's the speed limit on this stretch?" asks Marjorie.

"Ah, don't worry," shrugs Tim. "They watch this highway pretty close, you can't get away with anything along here."

Marjorie and I tighten our seatbelts. For a long time, our van is stuck behind a tiny car, which is belching blue smoke, stuck behind a massive truck. Every so often the tiny car pulls out into oncoming traffic, hovers there for a moment, then pulls back in behind the truck, usually just in time to avoid a head-on collision.

"Oh, for God sake!" snaps Delia. "Somebody ought to give that guy a ticket!"

"They certainly should," agrees Marjorie through clenched teeth.

Delia turns to her, incensed. "Can you imagine? A trucker like that who don't pull off the road and give the little guy a chance? Oughta have his license removed!"

"What are those for?" asks Jack, pointing to fences that run alongside the highway.

"Probably protection," answers Genevieve. "From those flash floods."

"Naw," says Lenore, disbelievingly. Genevieve fixes her with a look.

"It's to keep the asses out," says Tim. Genevieve blanches.

"Did y'all say asses?" asks Delia. "What do y'all mean by that?"

"Asses, wild donkeys," says Tim. "They get on the road, make a hell of a mess with a car. Some towns—like Searchlight up ahead—they walk right down the main street."

"Get your camera, Geegee," says Delia. "You can take a picture a' one a' those donkeys."

Genevieve is already rummaging in her purse. "Yeah, I could send a postcard home. An ass for an *ass!*" She barks with laughter. Delia joins in. Lenore smiles vaguely. Marjorie purses her lips and looks away.

When we get to Searchlight, Tim pulls in at a roadside restaurant. The Star Sisters rush off to buy snacks. Jack and Tim and I step out to stretch our legs. Marjorie waits in the van. Tim launches into a lesson about the history of mining in the area, Searchlight in particular. Looking out at the desert, the arid sand stretching in every direction. It seems an utterly strange, uncomfortable place. I see nothing that resonates in my soul. I wonder at Tim's enthusiasm for it. I glance back at Marjorie waiting in the van. She sits, looking forlorn. It's clearly the last place in the world she'd like to be. Jack is grinning, fascinated by the story Tim is telling. During World War II, Tim says, Searchlight was an important Coast Guard station.

"You're kidding!" gasps Genevieve. The Star Sisters have returned, slurping from large fountain drinks and chomping at cinnamon buns the size of serving platters.

"This is one helluva sweetie pie," says Delia, sucking noisily at her fingers. "Lenore. You bring any more napkins?" Lenore goes back inside. "Thanks, honey!" Delia calls after her. "What's that? Coast Guard? Is there an ocean around here?"

Tim winks at Jack and me. "Searchlight," he continues, "is where General Patton's troops trained on Ships of the Desert."

"SHIPS? In the DESERT?" Delia's incredulous.

Tim nods. "Of course, you all know that's what they called camels. Right here's where they trained the first camel troops."

As we travel along down the highway, Marjorie keeps a

watchful eye on the road ahead. Jack and I are absorbed in the passing landscape, the ladies absorbed in their snacks. It strikes me that you'd have to be self-sufficient in every way, or a little crazy, to survive out here in this overwhelmingly empty space.

"I guess," says Jack thoughtfully after a while, "you could probably die out here."

The Star Sisters look at him.

"Jack." Marjorie whacks his knee.

"Yeah. Yeah, you could," agrees Tim. "It's a pretty powerful place, the desert."

Sobered, the ladies put away their snacks.

"But I love it," Tim goes on. "I love it. This is my home. There's no place like it on earth. Look at that!" he exclaims, pointing. We're descending into the Colorado River valley towards Laughlin. The view across the valley to the mountains of Arizona is spectacular.

"Check that out!" says Tim. "Isn't that something? Up in those hills," he continues, pointing towards Arizona, "there's special things in those hills."

"Like what?" I ask. Jack leans forward eagerly.

"Well," says Tim. "Up in those hills... is where the space ships land." He smiles at us in his rearview mirror. I glance around at my fellow passengers. No one blinks.

"Pardon?" I say.

"Yeah. Oh, yeah. You haven't heard?" For the briefest moment I think he's joking. "Yup, this is a pretty famous landing spot. Up there, and over there, and up there, too." He points in different directions. "People come from all over to go up in the ships."

The Star Sisters are staring at Tim, blank-faced. I don't dare look at Marjorie.

"You should check it out," Tim continues. "There's alot of famous people been up in those ships. Like Jimmy Carter, for one. Did you know that?"

"No," I say. "I'm not too familiar with UFOs."

"Oh yeah, and lots of other celebrities, politicians. Check the internet, it's all there."

"Have you," I hesitate. "Have *you* ever been up in a space ship, Tim?"

The ladies' jaws drop. Their eyes are wider than flying saucers.

"No, I haven't," answers Tim. "Not yet. But maybe one day, if I'm lucky."

We've arrived in Laughlin. Tim pulls up at the first hotel and turns to us.

"The way I see it," he says softly, "is that out there is nine planets, and beyond those nine planets" —he stretches his arms wide— "is the Mother Ship. And this Mother Ship, she's sending out shuttles in every direction." His fingers flick this way and that. "And one of these days, I hope to be there when one of those shuttles lands. And I'll get on it, I will. I'd really like to."

The Star Sisters are frozen in their seats. I look at Jack. He's frowning and rubbing his hands together, obviously uncomfortable with this information. I look at Marjorie...and do a double take. Marjorie, prim and proper Marjorie, is beaming back at Tim with a light in her eyes.

"Well, come on, ladies!" chirps Tim, leaping out. "Your stop!"

The Star Sisters start as if waking, and scramble out of the van as fast as they can, without goodbyes. Tim hops back in and we carry on to my hotel, the *Pioneer*. Jack's still frowning at his hands, turning them over and over in his lap. I say goodbye to him and Marjorie and climb out of the van. As I wait for Tim to unload my suitcase, there's a tap on my shoulder. It's Marjorie.

"I just wanted to say," she says, "it was nice sharing the trip with you."

"Yes, it was," I smile back, surprised.

"And..." She hesitates, checking over her shoulder to see if Jack is listening. "And what he was saying. About the space ships? I..." She glances at Jack again. "It's all true," she whispers. She takes my elbow, pressing it gently. "It's *all true*," she says again, with meaning. "I just wanted to tell you that." She puts her finger to her lips.

As the van drives away, I stare after it. Marjorie. Who'd have thought?

Much later, in the relative cool of the evening, I join the promenade on the boardwalk that runs along behind the hotels above the Colorado River. Couples stroll past me arm in arm, jiggling their pots of quarters and gazing up into the night sky. I make my way to the water's edge and crouch there in the darkness. Stars wink down at me in patterns that I recognize from home, muting the sense of strangeness I felt traveling over the desert earlier today. In the blackness, the desert doesn't even seem to exist. I study the stars carefully, trying to spot one that's different from the rest, one that might be a shuttle from the Mother Ship looking for a place to land. I wonder if Tim or Marjorie are standing somewhere in the darkness too, watching and waiting.

About the author:

Born in Baltimore, Maryland, and raised in Edmonton, Alberta, Karin Konoval currently lives in Vancouver, British Columbia. Her writing has been published in *Exact Fare Only II* (Anvil Press), *Other Voices* (Alberta Literary anthology), *Playboard Magazine*, and *The Courier*. Her work has been broadcast on CBC's *First Person Singular*, *Radio 3*, and *Alberta Anthology*. As a professional actor, Karin has appeared in lead roles at theatres across Canada, and received many honors for her work, most notably in musical theatre. On screen, she has appeared in principal and guest-starring roles in TV series such as *X-Files*, *The Dead Zone*, *Stargate*, and many others. Her numerous feature film credits include, most recently, the role of Mary Leonard in *Cable Beach* for which she won a Philip Borsos award.

Our
Favorite
Authors
Section

TIGER ROSE
©2004 by Elizabeth Appell

On the cold blustery afternoon that Tiger Rose died, she rocked her oak chair harder and faster than she ever had before, because she sensed the approach of the evil sensations that indicated the Devil was near. She knew she had the strength for one more go round with that out-and-out rotter and, for darn tootin' sure, it was gonna be a good whamdoozie.

Setting on the dilapidated porch of the likker hut, she acknowledged, *At ninety-five, Tiger Rose, you ain't so strong no more, but you still a smart one.*

Just the thought of the skirmish to come stirred the juices in her soul and supplied her with just enough grit to do two things: finish her last batch of prime moonshine and figure out how to beat the Devil at his own game. It weren't that she worried so much about her entrance into the next world, but she sure would like to exit this one in a way that'd give the good old boy a run for his money.

So, before going to the burying ground where she knew the scrap would be waged, she first tended the fire in the likker hut. For over an hour she fed the flames with logs of last spring's Maple. The bootleg boiled and bubbled in the very same pot her daddy had made 'shine in.

With the fire stoked, Tiger Rose fell heavily into the porch rocker and watched the plume of wood smoke fan out of the still's chimney. Its musky scent wafted toward the blue Kentucky

Mountains. She raised her face, her nose sniffing cat-like at the air. It weren't only wood smoke she smelled. There was a distinct scent of devilish provocations in the atmosphere. She sensed in her gut that that old son of a bitch was about to come a courtin' and that meant she'd have to deal with him direct on. She leaned her head against the chair back and started rocking to the same rhythm of the wind.

Sure enough, them sensations started up again.

They came from the burying ground: a sweet odor of decay and a sound of ancient metals scraping together deep in the earth. She set her jaw. *I ain't afeard of him.* Familiarity had toughened her.

Feeling more brittle than a frozen twig, she wended her way over to the family cemetery just about spitting distance from the hut. Headstones stuck out of the hard ground like bookmarks, noting the place where her dear mama lay, as well as that of her daddy. Another marked the resting place of her husband Emelly. Four more stood nearby and on those were carved the names of her four children: Fagan, Cunvelyn, Annest and Owain.

As she inched herself onto a stone bench that would be her marker, a chill dug deep into her bones and gouged mean at her joints. Her name was finely chiseled with the date of her birth: June 14, 1909, followed by a dash. She doubted that when her time came, anybody would get around to filling in the final date of her life in this world. If they did, she would hiss at them from the beyond, *You ain't got time to hack at that old stone on my behalf, and if you do, you should be shot!*

Setting on her bench, she smelled the foul odors of decay and heard the screeching sounds until she could stand it no longer. She put her hands over her ears and let it fly: *You red ant slime! You larvae pus!*

Long ago, she had discovered it worked real good against the dark force if she took to describing the nasty foulness that crawly things made. But now, stringing the cuss words together came hard and that was just another signal that her dying time hovered close.

Tiger Rose had lived with the Devil nudging at her from the day she pushed into this world. Over and over her mama had told Tiger Rose the story about her birthing day.

"From the moment my labor had begun, everything went off kilter," Mama would say. Her mama's eyes would fill when she told the part about how Tiger Rose's daddy was in the birthing room, standing next to Midwife Vaughn Jones and how he had grunted and moaned as if he were the one delivering. Then her daddy started breathing deeper and ran his fingers lightly over his belly exactly as a woman would do to tickle away the pain.

Mama said that she had pushed like a rooting pig to get Tiger Rose, her second girl, out of her body, and when the midwife saw that the baby had crowned, her face lit up like Tittle Click Glen under a starry midnight.

"Your baby's head looks like a red sunset with dark stripes crossing its skies," said Midwife Vaughn Jones and then she handed her mama a mirror so she could see the top of the infant's mop showing through that vaginal window. That was when Midwife Vaughn Jones tugged the baby out, a squalling thing with a wet and gluey crop of hair that looked more like it belonged to a baby tiger. When her daddy saw the small, striped head and beneath it a flushed face the color of a late summer flower, he wept and called out, "My Tiger Rose!" That's when her name took form.

And then Midwife Vaughn Jones held Tiger Rose up. Low and behold, Tiger Rose was covered with a wispy shawl, a veil like a spider's web. Her mama told her that when Midwife Vaughn Jones, who passed on now over thirty years ago, saw that veil, her face turned dark. Midwife Vaughn Jones cleaned up the baby quick as could be, rubbing off that stringing mess and tossing it into the fire. She wrapped Tiger Rose in a rough, clean blanket, pressed her into her mama's arms and left the house without turning back. Her mama said that she and Tiger Rose's daddy sat holding Tiger Rose in silence for the worry about what the veil meant took away their words. Mama said all that was heard in the small wooden house was the tick-tock of the wind-up clock and the beating of the new baby's heart.

That night Tiger Rose's daddy joined the rag-tag men of neighboring hollers in raising more than one mug of 'shine to celebrate the borning, though she would have bet her gold tooth that he never mentioned the veil, and it was after the third jar of brew he claimed that he had found blood in his britches. When Tiger Rose's mama told that part of the story she winked at Tiger Rose for she was no fool about the things men say when they swayed from the glories of moonshine.

The day Tiger Rose started female-type bleeding was the first day she got an inkling of the burden the veil carried. The moment she found blood in her cottons she immediately felt a close, hot breath nearby. She told her mama who nodded like she was expecting it, and her mama told Tiger Rose that when you bleed you're open. "Open to the two-step dance of the devil," she had said. Not knowing the consequences, Tiger Rose's sister jealously would tell how she too had been born with the veil, but mama assured Tiger Rose that she was the only one who'd came through the birthing window curtained in lace.

The day before she turned thirteen, Tiger Rose heard strange sounds like a squeaking rope tied tight round wood when her mama raised water from the well and that night she slept with pillows over both ears. The next evening, she heard the sounds again, but they were muffled by her daddy's sweet words when he said, "My Tiger Rose is a beauty all right, corn-tall with blue eyes round as plates and her bones angulated."

All through that evening the sounds kept pestering her, but they took a back seat when the air cracked with the explosion. Her daddy, under the swoon of 'shine and bent with the dread of descending one more time into the coal mine, had curled around his deer rifle and shot himself dead in the likker hut. Her daddy was her first lost and the weight of her sadness caused her to bow beneath it like a tree heavy with rain.

When she turned fourteen, she told her mama the sensations included smells like animal fat past its prime and a feeling of being wrapped in a grimy cotton cloak.

"Careful," Tiger Rose's mama warned her. "When you talk of such things they best be true because lying would open you a hundred times more than the bleeding days. You might as well fling wide the door and give the Devil an invite."

In the early part of her life, the sensations pestered Tiger Rose to distraction and she begged her mama to tell her what to do.

Her mama had never experienced the sensations herself, but she knowed no life passed without a dance or two with the Demon, so she did her best to teach the girl how to ward off the devilish aggravations.

Her mama had said that when them sensations pestered her, Tiger Rose should cling to the crucifix. Her mama showed her how to press the cross hard against her forehead. Next she told Tiger Rose to raise her voice in prayer. She had suggested that she bellow like a banshee so if God was busy elsewhere, he'll stop whatever he was doing and take notice of her.

During the summer solstice of her fifteenth year, her mother took her (Sister had run away with a tinker the month before) to the Eisteddfod Festival. The infectious rhythms of the two-four music played on the handmade harps and fiddles caused Tiger Rose's fingers and toes to dance on their own. That's where she got her first blink of Emellyn Williams. Tiger Rose couldn't take her eyes off the tall, gawky man who spoke strong and, with his roughened hands animating the tale, recited from memory the ninety-nine verses of the *Gododdin*. Tiger Rose and Emellyn married before Christmas.

Emellyn Williams carried a decade and a half on her and, like her daddy, he was a good but simple man who worked in the coal mine. Consequently, he coughed blood, saw life through only one eye due to an accident when a shot of iron seam scraped his cornea, and could barely read at the level of a fifth grader. He didn't believe in the devil nonsense and never put a token of credit in the fact that his wife and their children were all born with the veil.

Emellyn hated it when the sensations took over his wife, so never did she press the cross hard to her face when her husband was nearby. Nor did she call out prayers as her mama had instructed. Instead she took to cursing the Demon.

You 'shine jar of old piss! she'd bellow when those drat sensations interrupted her tasting as she seasoned a rabbit stew. If they interfered with her listening for her children to come skipping down the weedy road lined with Primroses and Trumpet Vine she'd wail, *Hold your mouth, you pile of pig pucky!*

As time went by, Tiger Rose refused to use the cross or even whisper a prayer to shun the Devil.

"The Devil's nothing to ignore, Tiger Rose," her mama would say.

It's not that Tiger Rose didn't understand that the sensations were taps on the shoulder from the Devil, but she had learned that she was strong enough on her own. One day, soon after the birth of her fourth child, Owain, Tiger Rose heard the infant choking. She ran to the crib and, sure enough, she could smell evil around the bed. The presence hovered, heavy and hungry, like a huge appetite fixing to gobble up anything that moved. She picked up her baby boy, clutched him as close to her breast as she could without squeezing the life out of the poor child, and then cussed something fierce, ordering the Devil to let her baby be and to take leave of her house. Her voice became hoarse before she felt the presence give in. As usual, she managed to summon up more stamina than it did, but after the confrontation, she collapsed and was left drained and empty for days.

Sometimes when the Devil diddled with her, to ignore him, she'd have to bite down hard enough to crack a molar. But there were other times when, if anyone was within a poke's throw, they'd know he was having his way. Her hands would shake, a thin trail of sticky drool would run out of her mouth, and she'd set out on a cursing rampage in a loud, raspy voice. During these times, Emellyn escaped to the still, fired up the cracking tower, and went to work producing a new batch of 'shine. Not until the episode had spent itself and her railing had ceased, would he return to the house, eyes fogged and talking like his mouth was chock full of cotton.

Once, when she cursed so loud and ferocious-like, her spit stung his face. Emellyn raised his hand with the intention of thrashing her, but he pulled back his blow. Later she touched him gentle and thanked him for not whopping her. She knew he knew she couldn't help it and she also knew he loved her the best he could. Besides, she cooked hardy, mended with clever stitches that couldn't be seen, patched a roof better than him, and hoarded money so good that one day they walked right into the Bank of West Virginia and on a shiny mahogany table laid down enough cash to buy their own acre. She understood that for him it wasn't so hard to balance the rifle on his legs and pull the trigger exactly like her daddy had done because he knew his lungs were crocheted with cancer and that his children were in good hands.

Her children grew up with barely a brush of the sensations. Now and then they noticed a putrid warm wind in the midst of an icy winter, or heard the scraping of metal against metal, a sound that would cause the hair on their arms to rise. Sometimes they felt pressure like a dark, foul blanket had been thrown over them. For the most part, however, they considered the sensations more like having a sniffle or a gouty day.

When it came to their mother's symptoms, they'd become accustomed to her shaking hands, drool running down her chin, or her eyes lighting up like Christmas globes. It was her foul cursing that they couldn't abide. As young'uns they'd turn scarlet with embarrassment. When grown, they explained their mother's behavior away by telling people she suffered fits. Once, she overheard Fagan telling the company store clerk that his mother had Tourette's. In the face of an episode, they'd abandon her, leaving her to stand alone exorcising the demon, the very one that haunted them.

She tried to get them to understand she did it for protection, but in truth, they thought her crazier than a holler witch.

Her protection weren't ever enough. As her children grew into adulthood, she understood that each of their weaknesses was the work of the Devil pressing down. He did so with such a heavy hand that, one by one, she buried them. Fagan, angrier than a pig smelling bacon, heard the sensations as he sailed into the darkness after swallowing a full bottle of sleeping tablets. She knew Cunvelyn smelled the Demon coming for him as he gulped his last wheezy snatch of air, a smoldering tip of a cigarette clutched between his yellowed fingers. Annest, who left fifty-three notebooks scrawled with inky pictures drawn in delicate wiggly lines, tasted the Demon as she convulsed due to a liver laden with 'shine. Owain felt him tinkering as his heart broke, pieces of it falling away due to a terrible sadness brought on when his wife of eight years died squeezing out a dead baby.

So, truth be known, Tiger Rose had always understood that the day would come when she no longer could go eye-to-eye with the Devil. She knew him a patient bugger who was waiting for her strength to fade and she had only one lifetime. He had forever.

That blustery day sitting on the stone bench, the one in the burying ground that would be her grave marker, she felt the air turn warm and she knew the Devil lurked nearby. As she ran her hand over the cold marble, she was ready. Her prime batch of 'shine was made, but how would she beat him at his own game?

A light rain began to fall. She stepped into it, moving from one grave marker to the next. She came to a small pond at the perimeter of the burying ground and looked in. For a split second her reflection shown between raindrops, a young face, laughing. And so the idea came to her.

That's it! She cried out. *I'm gonna beat you, you slick maggot of slime!*

As usual, the foul smells polluted the air and the deep scraping groans took to groaning and she started to laugh. She hooted and hollered and then cawed until tears ran down her face. The harder she laughed, the more agitated the force became. Laughter kept pushing out causing her to snort and gulp for air. Giggles erupted, turning into lively crows and hilarious cackles.

The presence bore down.

If you kill me, I'm surely gonna die laughing!

She kept on laughing and wiped tears from her eyes. The presence overtook the wind and caused it to roar with such ferocity, she couldn't hear her own bellowing. The sky filled with dirty clouds that blacked out the sun. Tiger Rose raised her hand but couldn't see it for the darkness. The sensations descended with all their force. Her stamina strained like a clothesline heavy with soaked sheets but she no longer could sustain the strength needed to wrestle the power. Disdainfully, Tiger Rose turned into the face of the wind and let it whip at her, for she was sure that once she entered the final darkness, she would be rid of the force forever. There would only be peace because during this life she had survived all the pain that had been earmarked for her.

As the sounds of glee escaped her throat, she turned round and round in a sort of waltz to music only she could hear. She laughed and danced, giddy as a young bride, whirling in circles that made her dizzy. The more she laughed, the stronger came the gusts. Her sides ached and her eyes reddened with tears. As she danced, the hot blasts of wind clawed at her white hair and whipped at her stained skirts. Despite the boiling fever singeing her skin, she continued erupting with joy.

Finally exhausted, she quieted. Ignoring the blistering scald, she curled up on her stone bench and closed her eyes. She knew if the Demon had its way, it would burn hotter than any fire she or her daddy had ever made in the still, and she would be nothing but a crisp of corn toast by morning. *Mama*, she whispered, *what do I do?* And she drifted into sleep.

At sunrise, a muscle-bound boy with hair combed with a greasy part knocked on the likker hut door. He had been sent by his daddy from Creepers Holler to buy a jar of 'shine. When no one answered at the hut, he looked around and there, in the small cemetery, he saw Tiger Rose curled on the stone bench. Stepping tentatively into the burying ground he inched up to her. She looked cold as the breath of Death, an ice lady. Her skin was translucent and a light, sweet odor of flowers emanated from her. He touched her gentle, like a bee collecting pollen, afeard that in death she'd break into a thousand pieces.

In her new world, at the whisper of the boy's touch, she opened her eyes to see a young man, a worthy escort for a fine lady. He reached out his hand and she took it. She rose and discovered she was covered by a veil and that she was strong and lithe. She entered his arms and he held her in dance position and she knew at any moment they would step into a dizzying polka to whirl wildly between the graves.

Tiger Rose looked up at the young man and smiled, not a faint smile with a narrowing of eyes that caused her lips to crease, or a shy, partial smile hinting at pleasure, but a broad, joyous smile that lay across her small, cold face, and spread from ear to ear in victory.

About the Author:

Elizabeth writes screenplays, plays and novels as well as short stories. Her first play, "Confessions of a Catholic Child" was a finalist in the Writer's Network Fiction Contest in Los Angeles, chosen for staged reading by The Long Beach Playhouse, finished fifth in a field of 9,000 in the 1998 Writer's Digest Playwriting Competition, and optioned by a Canadian producer to create a one-hour film based on the play. Her second play, "Moon Walkers" finished second out of a field of 300 in the Do Gooder Productions New Playwright Award Competition, was recognized as a semi-finalist in Writer's Network 1998 competition, was part of New Theatre Works Festival 99 in Santa Rosa, became a semi-finalist in the Writer's Network Screenplay & Fiction Competition and placed in the top ten plays out of a field of 19,000 in the October 2000 Writer's Digest Writing Competition. Her "Journal of a Common Man," won Dominican University's Festival of Short

Plays. Elizabeth's fourth novel, "Lessons From the Gypsy Camp' was published by Scribes Valley Publishing in 2004.

TOBY AND BEAU

©2001 by Gail Cauble Gurley
from Tales From the Sunroom
Used here by special permission of the author
©2001 by Gail Cauble Gurley

Friendship gives for the sheer joy of the gift,
asking no payment.
--g. gurley

He pulled his pocket watch out, and checked it as the clock in the church tower on the square struck one.

"Come on, Beau, let's go eat," he called, as he pulled himself out of his chair.

Soon he was stepping off the walkway, standing at the edge of the cobblestone street, waiting for two horse drawn carriages to pass. Beau sat patiently at his feet, his tiny bright eyes following the horses as they clopped by. He jumped to his feet, wagging his tail excitedly as Toby exchanged greetings with one of the drivers, but the tiny dog did not move until Toby started across the street, signaling to Beau that it was safe to continue.

Toby pushed open the door to the Korner Kitchen, held it for Beau, then closed it behind them. Each head in the pub lifted, and each faced was crossed with a smile as warm phrases greeted the duo. Several patrons leaned over to scratch behind Beau's ears, and Mazie came from behind the counter with a small treat for her favorite customer.

Al, the cook, shouted an exuberant, "'Ello," and threw a link of sausage in the pan for their tiny guest.

In 1856 London, no one objected to a small dog in a pub, especially one as well behaved as Beau. He had been a daily fixture at the establishment since Toby found him abandoned, cold and hungry, five years earlier. His brilliant black eyes were barely visible through the mass of hair exploding over his face, but even those thick curls could not hide the intelligence in that miniature frame, nor could they hide the love and devotion he had for Toby.

Each day for as long as most of them could remember, Toby McLauren had eaten lunch at the Korner Kitchen. He and his wife had been childless, and she had died fifteen years earlier after a five-year illness.

Toby was a giant of a man who had worked as a blacksmith until an accident with a wench severed his hand six years ago. He possessed a quiet and gentle dignity in sharp contrast to his muscular size. He would literally fill a door with his mass; yet nearly disappear after entering a room. His dignified unpretentiousness allowed him to enjoy his privacy without being reclusive. He was, however, quite approachable and deeply respected by his neighbors and fellow Londoners, who had known him both as a blacksmith and a friend.

Toby had been lonely following the death of his wife, and had thrown himself into his work. His metal fence work, stair rails, balusters, and decorative ironwork were widely accepted and prized by those fortunate enough to attain them. His greatest work, however, was a high, intricate fence enclosing the front of the two hundred year old cemetery just a few blocks from his small home and the Korner Kitchen. The thin rods of iron were twisted, bent and molded into beautiful, complex designs almost lacelike in their delicacy, but the design promised to exist timelessly as long as it was cared for. The most breathtaking section was the huge double gate covering the entrance to the three-acre site. It represented Toby's concept of the tree of life, and spread majestically to the top corners, with branches reaching and cascading thickly to the edges of the sides and leaping above the top frames, like fingers reaching for heaven in determination not to be confined within borders. The massive, textured trunk supporting the thick limbs and branches was split in half as the door opened. Each door was twenty-five feet wide and caused people to shake their heads in wonder as to how something so substantial could stand so solidly and open so easily.

He had begun work on the project shortly before his wife's illness. It grew and evolved as her illness progressed and became a love letter to her spirit. After her death, he worked with even more dedication and purpose, and had completed the gate and five hundred feet across the front when he had his accident. The fence represented twelve years of imagination, planning and artistry.

The directors of the cemetery decided to complete the project with a stonewall connecting each end of Toby's fence so as to enclose the remaining property. The city was disappointed that his work was incomplete, but the thick, solid stones enhanced and complemented the airiness of the ironwork, and gave the cemetery coziness and comfort, which were non-existent before Toby's work had begun. It became a prestigious, as well as historic area, with people coming from near and far to view the beauty of the fence.

Each day after finishing their meal, the two friends would walk to the cemetery, and Toby would sit by his wife's grave, quietly reflecting, smoking his beloved pipe. Beau would lie under a huge marble coffin next to the gravesite. The coffin set on twenty-four inch high piers placed under each corner of the box. The epitaph read, "He thought he was a head above everyone else."

Toby had chuckled the first time he saw it, but it became a very nice place for Beau to rest away from the weather and pesky insects that pervaded the city.

Toby and Beau became fixtures in the area, and people derived great comfort from seeing them on their daily sojourn. Beau's loyalty to his master and Toby's devotion to his wife's memory were heartwarming. Their presence seemed to bring order and peace to the day.

It was a beautiful, bright day in early June. Even the normal smoky soot from countless chimneys was thinner that day. Mazie looked up as the tower clock in the church struck one.

"Toby and Beau will be 'ere soon," she commented.

Al reached over for a thick piece of ham he'd saved that morning. He received great pleasure in feeding the gentle little Beau.

'E'll like this, he thought, as he slapped it in the pan.

Time passed and Mazie became concerned.

"They should be 'ere by now." She couldn't hide her worry.

"Maybe they just got delayed." Al was trying to hide his own uneasiness.

Mazie waited a few minutes more, and then moved across the floor to peep anxiously out the door. No sign of them anywhere. An hour later, she could wait no longer. She removed her apron.

"I'm going looking for 'em."

Al shouted as she exited, "Wait up! I'll go with ya." He locked the door of the empty pub on his way out.

They knocked on the door of Toby's small house but received no answer. They knocked louder and Mazie called out. Beau barked from inside, and they exchanged a brief glance before Al forced the door open.

Beau met them in the hall, barking anxiously, and ran to the back of the house. They followed and before they could get there, he ran back to them, barking insistently and impatiently.

"Awright, awright, old boy, we're coming!"

As they entered the dark bedroom, Mazie scooped Beau up and held him close. Al checked the motionless form on the bed, and shook his head sadly at Mazie.

"Oh, no!" she moaned, and buried her face in Beau's trembling fur.

She took the small dog home with her, determined to care for him just as Toby had. Beau cried pathetically, pacing endlessly before the door of her flat, begging to be released. She took him out on a leash as she feared he would run away to Toby's home and be injured in some way.

She tied him to a bench in the pub while she worked. He would leap up, wiggling exuberantly each time the door opened, but would lie down in deep disappointment when Toby didn't enter.

The day of the funeral arrived and Toby was laid to rest beside his beautiful Harriet. The gates he so lovingly created opened, and Toby entered for the last time. Beau trotted beside the casket and lay by it as the services were conducted. When it was time to leave, he refused to go. Mazie managed to capture him and carry him back to the pub.

As she entered, Beau wriggled free, and fled out the door. She bolted after him but was no match for his determination as he escaped. She found him lying on top of Toby's grave.

"Okay, little fellow," she stated kindly. "I understand. This is where you need to be right now so just stay. I'll keep an eye on you and make sure you don't go 'ungry.'"

The tower clock struck one that afternoon and Mazie looked up out of habit, then sadly realized her error. She went back to her chores and stopped when she heard a familiar bark at the door.

Beau bounded in when she opened it and was soon eating ravenously. He had refused to eat until now and was quite hungry.

As soon as he finished eating, he returned to the door, and looked up imploringly at Mazie. She smiled resignedly, opened the door and released Toby's tiny guardian. Beau rushed out, and she was certain he would return to the cemetery. Just to reassure herself, she stopped by that evening on her way home from work. Sure enough, there he was, resting quietly on top of Toby's grave.

He raised his head and wagged his tail briefly but made no effort to move from his sentinel spot. She placed a small bowl of water under the stilted marble casket near Toby's grave, turned to go, and blew Beau a kiss.

"G'night, Beau. See you tomorrow?"

Beau's bright eyes followed her as she left, then he dropped his head between his front paws and settled down for the night.

Each day shortly after the one o'clock announcement from the tower, Beau would return to the Korner Kitchen for his one meal of the day. Immediately upon completing his repast, he returned to his master in the cemetery. Just as faithful, Mazie would take fresh water to Beau daily, and when winter arrived, she placed warm hay beside the water, hoping to entice him to leave his hallowed spot to escape the cold.

She was encouraged when she found him between the piers, under the casket on several cold afternoons.

Winter passed, then another and another. Three years after Toby's death, Harvey Gray, a new director, arrived at the cemetery. He was young with very modern and conservative views.

He was appalled by Beau's presence, and immediately attempted to chase him away. Beau, however, was having no part of it, and Director Gray chased him for several hours on that first day he became aware that Beau was an unwelcome resident. They ran in and out, around and behind the many monuments. Gray caught his toe on a partially submerged footstone and fell sprawling across the graves. He scrambled up, cursing and fuming, while Beau scooted under a thick hedge for safety.

Gray lost sight of Beau when he fell and spent several minutes searching for the tiny fugitive; finally deciding he had succeeded in chasing him away. He limped off, rubbing his knee, muttering under his breath about the filthy beast that had invaded *his* cemetery.

Mazie was alarmed that evening as she arrived at the cemetery, and discovered that Beau was not at his usual spot on the grave or under the casket nearby. She called him softly, and soon heard a rustling in the bushes. Beau slipped out, wriggling happily at her feet.

"What's the matter, fella? Huh? Are you okay?" She soothed him as she rubbed his ears.

For several days, she discovered him in a similar state. She worried about him and mentioned her concern to Mitchell, the police Bobby in their area, as he was eating there one noon. Beau arrived for his meal while Mitchell was still there. Mazie approached him, rubbing his ears as she always did. He flinched and drew back from her touch.

"What's that?" she questioned, as her hand touched something hard on his head. She checked and discovered dried blood on a small cut.

"Mitchell, it's blood!" Mazie was visibly shaken.

"Go ahead and feed 'im, Mazie, and I'll follow him when he leaves. Something's afoot."

Mitchell followed him from the pub. Beau stopped at the cemetery gate, glanced furtively about, and then dashed into the cemetery, darting behind stones and peeking out nervously before advancing to the next one, until he made his way to his beloved destination.

Strange, thought Mitchell. *He acts like someone's chasing him.*

Mitchell stood back out of sight and quietly watched. Shortly, he heard a shout and Beau leaped up, scampering away. Harvey Gray appeared, a large stick in his hand, and began to chase Beau.

"'Ey, there, what are you doing?" demanded Mitchell.

Gray stopped short, obviously startled. As he saw the Bobby, he dropped the stick and began to sputter in confusion.

"That dog has no business here, and I won't have him in my cemetery!"

Mitchell moved toward him slowly, and spoke softly but with authority.

"'E was here before you were, Mr. Gray, and 'e's doing nobody no harm. I'm warning you to leave 'im alone. If anything happens to him, I'll hold you personally responsible. And you don't want to deal with the good folks of this community if you hurt old Beau."

"We'll just see about that," Gray sputtered. "I'll let the directors know he's here and they'll get rid of 'im, I'll wager. I was trying to be kind and run him off but the board may not be so charitable."

"Well, in the meantime, you've been warned not to harm the little bugger."

Mitchell stayed until Gray stormed off, and Beau came out of hiding. He comforted the little dog, and then he returned to the pub to make a report to Mazie.

She was livid and immediately began plotting her strategy to fight Harvey Gray. Fortunately, Al served on the board of directors at the cemetery so she knew she and Beau had at least one ally. He soothed Mazie as he promised to do all he could. He did share with her that none of the board members had ever complained or received a complaint that he knew of against Beau's being in the cemetery. Actually, several members had verbally praised the little dog for his loyalty and dedication. They found it both inspiring and touching in a sometimes cold, unfriendly world.

At Harvey Gray's request, a special meeting of the board was called within the week. He strode arrogantly, confidently into the room and was met with cold, hard stares from the board as well as several angry citizens. These stares immediately took some of the starch out of his sails.

Within thirty minutes of his entrance, he sat angrily trembling, flushed and dry mouthed, before the group. They were firm and stanch in their decree that Beau stay at his chosen assignment.

He leapt up and cried passionately, "Either that dog goes or I do!"

He was met with stony silence, and felt the color drain from his face as he realized what had just happened. He struggled to regain a degree of dignity before making a hasty retreat.

"Let's remember this when we get a new director," Al remarked. "We'll tell 'im that Beau stays."

The room erupted in applause and happy shouts. Mazie was particularly relieved and grateful to all the board, especially Al.

And so, it was that Beau did stay for six more years. He began moving very slowly, his once bright eyes clouded with cataracts, and he took longer to arrive for lunch than he had in the past, but the entire neighborhood kept an eye on him so that he was able to cross the street safely. Mazie visited him each and every evening with a gentle pat and kind word. Beau was quite the hero.

The inevitable day came when the fifteen-year-old dog didn't appear for lunch. Mazie looked up and met Al's eye. Neither spoke as she slipped her scarf over her head and exited the pub.

Al removed his apron, following close behind her. Soon a small, sad group gathered behind them as they all moved toward the McLauren Memorial Cemetery.

Mazie gently picked up the tiny body lying on top of his master's plot, burying her tearful face in his graying curls. The men removed their hats and the women wept into their handkerchiefs.

Two days later a large crowd gathered at Toby's gravesite. The priest at the tower church officiated as they prepared to scatter Beau's ashes over Toby's grave. Mazie and Al could not bring themselves to bury him away from this site, and even the compassionate board of directors couldn't grant permission to bury him there so a compromise had been to have him cremated and spread his ashes.

They waited silently for the church clock to strike one, as Mazie had requested. As it did, Father Rogers spoke of Beau's loyalty and faithfulness.

"Beau possessed attributes elusive to even most humans. He was more than a friend—he became a guardian angel. He entered Toby McLauren's life at the depth of human grief and loneliness, and remained by his master's side, even after Toby's death. Beau was on earth a scant fifteen years, but he has touched many, as few humans living much longer are able to do. Beau is now with his beloved Toby, and they will be together forever. Rest well, thou true and loving servant."

After those few brief, eloquent words, Mazie lovingly scattered Beau's ashes over Toby's grave and stepped away. Each mourner tossed flowers on the spot—some had one or two and others had bouquets. Soon the area was covered with colorful offerings. It eased their pain and celebrated little Beau's existence among them. He had made a difference in their world.

Several months later, a local budding sculptor who had befriended Beau, pulled a wagon with a large, covered package into the pub and presented it to Mazie.

"I'd like for you to have this in memory of Beau. It seems tragic that he was so important to this community for there not to be something to mark his passage through our lives."

He removed the canvas covering, and there was a beautiful, black marble statue of Beau, gazing back at them. His curls wound and cascaded down the figure and over his face. His tiny eyes appeared bright and sharp, even though they were of stone. His mouth was open in an enthusiastic breath with his tiny tongue furled out excitedly, and he was perched on his hind legs, as he did while at Toby's feet.

"Oh, William," Mazie gasped emotionally, "it's lovely! 'E looks so real!"

Her obvious pleasure and gratitude warmed him, and made him glad that he had created this work. The little creature had mattered, and now all of time would know.

The statue set in a place of honor at the pub until Al and Mazie were able to get permission to place it on a pedestal at the head of Toby's grave.

"'E'll be here forever, with his good friend, Toby," Al decreed as they set the figure in place.

About the author:

Gail published a collection of inspirational short stories entitled *Tales From the Sunroom* in 2001. It has been well accepted and acclaimed. Her new novel entitled *The Bird House: A Gift of Hope* was released in December, 2002. It is an inspirational story of a young family in New York during the Great Depression and their struggles to survive. Reviews on this latest work have been excellent. She resides in North Carolina with her husband of 32 years. They have a daughter and three grandchildren in Houston, TX. She earned a B. A. in psychology and an M. Ed in education from the University of North Carolina at Greensboro. Writing has been the realization of a lifelong dream, and she credits her success to the encouragement and support she has received from her family and many friends.

A PROMISE IS A PROMISE
©2005 by Carolyn Ann Aish

Wearing a deep frown that pleated his handsome brow, Crown Prince William Charles paced a few steps one way then the other. At the sound of footsteps on the northern staircase, he strode to the rail to see who was coming. Disbelief clouded his countenance and he stepped to the top of the staircase, waiting for the lithe young man to surface. The moment the 'felon' stepped foot cn the top step, William Charles accosted him. Grabbing him by both sides of his tunic collar, with a good amount of fabric clutched in his royal hands, the Prince, his face reddening, shook the young man. As his victim, one hand on the rail, stepped backwards, the Prince pushed him across the marble floor.

"What are you doing up here, jester Lester? Get back where you belong!" Swinging around, he pushed Lester towards the top step and released him with a shove.

Righting his balance so that he did not fall down the stairs, Lester ignored the unfathomable pain he felt and dusted himself in an exaggerated manner. With both hands, he pretended to put his head the right way around, making a gravelly sound, and swishing saliva through his teeth. Catching mirth on the faces of the guards and the two messengers, Lester grinned widely. He would have stepped around the prince, but the latter, with clenched fists, barred his way.

Lester spoke fast, "The King himself called me, Your Highness. The messenger said I must be here at two hours before noon. It's now after eleven. I've been returning back and forward for an hour already." Stepping sideways he strode quickly backwards before stopping at a safe distance to bow.

The Prince's face changed, but only to show more rage. He spoke through clenched teeth, "I am visiting with His Majesty, my brother. Perhaps you'll be permitted to keep your appointment, but only after I've seen him. Keep your distance, you witless clown. I'll not have you waiting close to my person. It makes me sick every time I see you."

Lester wished he could proclaim just how ill *he* felt to be close to the crown prince, but he kept silent and obeyed, allowing a large space between where the prince waited and where he stood at the other end of the long balcony. When he dared, he shot a glance at the prince, wondering as always why so much hate was bound within this royal person. It affected him in such a gut-wrenching way. He knew that the prince's hate was more than anger at the world; it was so much more personal than that.

The doors to the King's sanctum were closed and guarded. Only when the King's Receptionist, Sir Daley, ordered the doors opened and called one's name would one be permitted to be escorted through.

The doors opened and from within the corridor, lines of captains exited, donning their helmets as they passed under the portal. They bowed to the Prince, some grinning or winking at the Jester. The crown prince's extreme dislike for servants was well known, in particular his loathing of this young man.

When the last captain had gone, Sir Daley called, "Lester the Jester."

Prince William Charles stepped quickly to the portal only to find two spears crossed in his face. "I will see my brother!" he demanded.

"You'll see King William Henry *after* Lester. You, Your Highness, do not have an appointment."

"If you allow this…that…fool to enter before your Crown Prince, Daley, you'll be sorry! Inform King William Henry that his royal brother is here. He *will* see *me*, first!"

Sir Daley hesitated then backed away. The doors closed. With a smirk on his face, the Prince paced back and forth, hurling abuse, almost reaching the place where Lester stood.

"You really think you are someone, don't you, Jester? Well you're no one, and never will be. Hear me, you redundant fool, you make me ill, sick to the pit of my stomach, I'd like to see you dead!"

Lester, trembling inwardly, stood resolute, not looking at the Prince, but keeping his eyes fixed on the floor in front of his feet. Clenching his fists, he hoped that the ball of bile he felt rising from his stomach would not cause him to vomit.

The Prince's body shook with emotion as he shouted, "I'm sick of you, Jester. Perhaps I'll put an end to your miserable life before I become fatally diseased by you!"

Sir Daley returned and announced, "His Highness, Crown Prince William Charles."

Smoothing his long hair, tied back with a velvet bow, the Prince strode through the open doors.

Lester rushed down the stairs, taking four in each leap, and ran out into the foyer. This had happened before; not right here, but near the King's sanctum. He looked for a vessel and saw a potted plant. Grasping the edges of the pot, he heaved uncontrollably until he had vomited his breakfast onto the soil at the base of the large palm. Spitting and shaking, he felt so wretched he wanted to lie down. It was some moments before he could gain control of himself and not just weep. Ignoring guards and palace staff who looked on him with both amusement and contempt, he strode to the gymnasium where the royal guards worked out. As an acrobatic juggler and jester, he was permitted to use the facilities. After a harsh workout, he sat a while before eating from the huge fruit bowls and sipping cold well-water.

When he returned to check if the Crown Prince was still in the King's auditorium and, finding he was, Lester said to the messengers, "I'll be in the library, fetch me when I'm called."

Another encounter with the Crown Prince was not on Lester's list for the day.

An hour passed before the Prince, his face darker than ever, exited from his visit with his brother. Sir Daley called, "Lester the Jester."

"I'll fetch him, Sir," a messenger said.

In the spacious Royal Library, Lester helped the curator and his pretty young niece replace borrowed books on the high shelves. Lester arranged the books in perfect order, slid deftly down the ladder, his moccasined feet outside the steel rails, and stood beside the girl of his dreams.

"You take my breath away when you do that, Lester," Julia whispered.

"I'd like to think I took your breath away for other reasons," Lester said, stepping closer. He encircled her with his arms and would have kissed her, but she drew back.

"Be careful, Uncle's here..."

"He's shelves away, and I only want one kiss."

"I want us to wait until we're betrothed."

"Then let me request your uncle now for your hand."

"I've told you. He believes I can do better."

"What do *you* think?"

"You know what I think, Lester. I want only you, but I want to do it right. Mother always said that when I choose someone, I must make sure I get it right. A lifetime is too long to have it wrong."

"You know that's what I want, too." He snatched her hand and kissed the back of it before saying, "Let's pledge ourselves to each other so that we know to whom we belong..."

"Without Uncle's permission?" she asked, her bright blue eyes looking even larger. "I'm not yet eighteen, Lester."

Shaking his head, Lester admitted, "You're right. We should wait. But you've no idea how hard it is." Lester leaned towards her and this time she did not pull away. Their lips met in a gentle, tender kiss. It was their first.

"You're so beautiful," Lester whispered.

"Do you really want to...marry me...be with me...forever?" she asked.

"No," he replied, his eyes not leaving hers.

"No? You're jesting, of course. You'd be sad if I walked away and we never saw each other..."

"No," he interrupted. His grip on her hands strengthened. Teardrops rose in her beautiful eyes and spilled down her cheeks as she closed her long eyelashes in sorrow. Blinking, he drew her closer, surrounding her with his strong arms.

"I don't just want to be with you forever, Julia. I *need* to be with you forever. I wouldn't just be sad if you walked away, I swear I'd die."

She smiled up at him. His lips met hers in a second, more serious kiss than the first, growing in intensity. They each could feel the other's heartbeat, as if they were one person.

"I want only you," Lester said, stopping to breathe, "I swear I'll marry you, only you, Julia. That's a promise!" He kissed her again.

"Lester?" the curator called, his voice sounding close. "Where are you, Lester. Julia?"

While Lester, breathing as if he had run a race, ascended the ladder as fast as he could, Julia, also gasping and red-faced, snatched up a pair of books and hurried around the end of the shelf, calling, "Here, Uncle, I'm here."

Lester moved along the top ramp before replying, "I'm up here, Sir Raven."

Five minutes later, Julia and Lester found each other again. No words were needed. They were in the middle of a very passionate kiss when a voice called, "Is Lester the Jester here? King William Henry will see him now."

Lester entered the King's sanctum and was ushered into the small throne room. A group of advisors, most of them wizened and ancient, stood to one side of the room, and a trio of scribes sat at their desks on the other.

As Lester bowed low, the King descended from his blue and white sapphire-studded throne. "We'll walk." King William Henry, dressed in his royal robes, the kingdom's crown on his head, embraced Lester's shoulders with one arm, drawing him towards a side door, which the guards opened. "Fresh air! What relief," the King said, as he pulled off his crown and placed it on a podium. A door along the corridor was opened. They stepped out on to a balcony.

"I've heard you're spending most of your time in the library, Lester."

"Yes, Sire."

"It's more than books."

"Yes, Sire."

"The curator's niece is beneath your station..."

Lester could not hold his thoughts and he exclaimed, "Beneath my station? Sir Raven believes Julia to be above *me*, Sire."

"Julia, daughter of the late Captain Raven, is beneath you, Lester. You will not court her. Take her as a bedmate, but don't consider marriage."

"My...bedmate? But, I am but a servant, Sire. She is the daughter of a captain and a niece of the curator. Is she not above me?"

"She's beneath you, Lester. You want her as a mistress?"

"I want marriage, Sire. We're made for each other. I want her as a wife!"

"It's out of the question, Lester. You will court Lady Victoria."

"Excuse me?"

"Lady Victoria is suitable."

"It's no secret, Sire, that Prince William Charles wishes to court Lady Victoria, and..."

"*You* will court Lady Victoria."

Lester's stomach twisted to a knot and his deepest fears threatened to surface. "The Crown Prince will hate me even more," he said as though to himself.

"Prince William Charles is to marry a Jiaryan princess. It will be arranged today. You will marry Lady Victoria."

Lester blurted, "Then, it's true? The late king was—my father? I'm a bastard child, the product of one of the late king's 'bedmates'?"

When the King did not answer but stared beyond the limits of the city, across the valley, into the distant mountains, Lester dared to ask, "Am I—your half-brother—Sire?"

Protests came from behind the pair and Lester realized they were not alone. The King's advisors had followed them to the balcony.

"You're not permitted to answer that question, Sire," the oldest of the advisors said firmly.

"Well?" the King asked, his eyes scalding them, "what do you advise?"

"Just as you said, Sire. Lester will *not* marry the book girl!"

"Lester deserves to know the reason..."

At that moment the door opened and a herald called, "Sir Seger, Ambassador of Jiarya awaits His Majesty."

"An hour late?" The King, his face dark, turned back to Lester. "Wait on us, Lester...or return in an hour. I'll expect a promise from you. You do remember those other promises?"

"Yes, Sire. I always keep my promises." Lester bowed and, as the King swept past, he vowed he would not make any more promises to the King, but he would keep the one he had made to Julia and marry her.

After telling the messengers he would be in the library, Lester mused, *Sir Raven won't let me marry Julia, and the King also refuses, but for opposing reasons. Who knows the truth? The King and everyone older than my twenty years know. Those behind-the-hand-whisperers, who laugh at my jesting, but look on me with knowing eyes, they know. I'm a bastard son of a dead king and have no rights, not in the upper class, nor in the lower class. No wonder Charlie hates me. He'd kill me before allowing me to share his royal father, and brother...*

Stepping into the library, Lester muttered to Sir Raven,

"Someone more important than me—which includes the whole world—arrived to see the King. Now, where was I?"

"Deliver these books to Sir Daley's quarters. His apple polisher will give you the returns."

"The King wants to see me again. A messenger will come..."

"Then hurry."

Lester's feet fairly flew as he made the delivery and soon he was back in the library. He longed to kiss Julia again, but she was working close to her uncle's desk, rearranging books on a lower shelf. Lester knew that the curator was watching closely and keeping Julia near him.

"Here, when you've checked those returns, these books need to be organized in chronological order in the history section, Jester. You'll need the ladder."

Lester sighed as he viewed six large chests of books. Testing the weight of one with a grunt, he unlatched it, lifted out an armful of books, and set to work.

Three chests were emptied before Julia called softly, "Uncle's stepped out, Lester."

With a quick slide down the ladder, Lester smiled and said, "Where were we?" After kissing until they were breathless, he said, "This is a good enough understanding for me, Julia. Promise me, no matter what anyone allows or disallows, you'll marry no one else."

"Uncle told me he knew you kissed me, but he wasn't mad about it, just...grim," she said, then quickly, "I promise."

Again their lips met.

The curator's voice called, "The messenger's here, Lester."

A voice called, "King William Henry is waiting on you, Jester."

"This way," called the messenger, leading in an opposite direction than before.

"Is the King not in his sanctum?"

"No."

Lester kept up with the young man as he wove through corridors unknown. They descended a narrow stairway and the messenger unlocked a small unguarded door and indicated that Lester enter.

"King William is in there?"

"King William *Henry*," the messenger corrected.

Lester felt he was the brunt of some kind of joke as he stepped through the door into the dim room. He felt a push from behind and he stiffened, on guard, his spine tingling from a nervous sensation that danger was near.

A quad of men leapt upon Lester and, although he fought them, he was rendered almost unconscious by a blow to his head with a blunt instrument. A bag was tied around his head and ropes were wound around his wrists and ankles.

"You knocked him out."

Lester's first thought was the King had arranged this fracas, then, he thought of the Crown Prince and his hatred. He struggled.

"Do it again."

Lester recoiled under another blow to the back of his head, and shuddered before forcing himself to go limp. A voice he knew, but could not place said, "Make sure there's no trace. Go to it then, and get back quick. It must be reported that none of you was out of the palace."

Lester was carried for a short time, and then thrown into what felt like a cart and covered with sacks. He knew he had little time, if any, to work out how to thwart these murderous plans and escape. He worked silently at the ropes on his hands, and somewhere in the back of his bruised head was the persistent thought, "Why? Why me?"

The men accompanying the cart stopped the vehicle on a long, wide bridge. Together they hoisted the bundle to the thick ledge, rolling it over to fall into the raging waters below. At the sound of a splash, they applauded.

Lester filled his lungs with air as he felt himself falling. It had taken all of his self-control not to reveal that he was conscious, and he decided he would rather face the river than try and fight the men who had already proven their strength. He was thankful they had not thrust a sword through him, or used their daggers to slit his throat.

The cold water engulfed him as he loosened the ropes around one wrist. The tumultuous currents buffeted him as he fought to surface, kicking and bucking with his bound feet. One hand came free and he pulled at the wet cloth over his face. The ropes around his neck, now saturated, tightened and he had the overwhelming sensation that he was going to drown. *God, I'm not ready to die!*

His life rolled quickly through his mind. He had been told that he was orphaned as a baby and was brought up in the servant's quarters in the royal palace. The term 'bastard child' was spoken often, and many times the Crown Prince himself had called Lester 'bastard'. He believed his mother to be a servant woman and his father a royal guard, but now he considered that perhaps the King was his father. He knew his parentage was a guarded secret, and it seemed obvious to Lester that his parents never married, and their affair, from which he was spawned, had been a clandestine one.

Lester grew up a sad and serious boy until, at the age of eight, he had seen a traveling band of jugglers and acrobatic comedians. He found telling jokes and performing as a jester was easy for him and, with much practice, he learned to somersault, tumble, and juggle at the same time. His crowning act was to juggle six flaming torches, making them appear as a circle of light in a darkened room. He had been applauded and cheered by the court. King William Henry had employed him as one of three official court jesters. Lester's humor was considered suitable for daytime entertaining and the younger guests in the early evenings, whereas the more adult humor came from the seasoned jesters.

Lester always believed the Crown Prince hated him because his jokes were too tame—the Prince's exploits with ladies often secretly gossiped about in the servant's quarters. Now that the King wanted Lester to marry the one whom William Henry desired would be reason enough for the Crown Prince to kill him.

As he struggled for air, Lester's thoughts flew to Julia. Beautiful, lovely Julia, the girl of his dreams and the one he wanted in his future. *I want to be her husband. I want a life with her. She's my other half. She'll complete me. I want to grow old with her. But now, it's ended. Life at the palace. Jesting. Juggling. Acrobatics. Reading and transcribing books in the library. Riddles from the King. Torment from the Crown Prince. Unanswered questions. The new curator and his niece, Julia...over before we've begun...Julia...she promised me, and a promise is a promise!*

With a rush, Lester surfaced and dragged in air, kicking at the water with his bound feet and legs. He struggled to stay afloat, but sank again and again. One wrist bore a wraith of rope, which dragged it down. He used the other hand, paddling to keep his head out of the torrent. Exhausted from battling against the strong undercurrents, Lester wondered if he could continue the fight.

Anger filled him when he thought of those who condemned him. William Charles had obviously planned it. Just this morning, he had threatened to kill him. Before he was dragged under again, he shouted, "Julia! A promise is a promise!"

Exerting every ounce of his strength, he wrestled for air before swirling with the waters, over rocks and down rapids. Soon, the waters slowed to a boil and, feeling battered and bruised, he marveled that he still lived and breathed.

The river washed him to the bank and he felt leaves and branches sweeping at him from above. He grabbed at the thick foliage, feeling glad. *Thank God!* he thought, then as he clung to the branches and pulled himself onto a solid bank, his thoughts said in more of a prayer-like manner, *Thank you, God. Thank you. You've saved me.*

Still half in the water, he hauled himself up, wanting to climb into the bushes overhanging the great river. The relentless current threw him against the hard bank spiked with rocks. Oblivious of the bruises and cuts, he dragged his cold body away from the moiling river to safety. Clawing at the brush and undergrowth, he wriggled further away from the breath-stealing foe, wishing he could free his ankles of the rope shackles, but the water had tightened their grip. On and on he writhed until he fell over a ledge of hard clay onto a firm floor. Collapsing, he lapsed into unconsciousness.

Julia was humming when the curator returned to the library. To her surprise, he joined in, humming the well-known folksong. Scarcely had five minutes passed when a messenger opened the library door and called, "Lester the Jester! The King requires that you complete your audience."

"But, he's already gone..."

"That's all right, Julia, I'll take care of this." Her uncle hustled the messenger out into the hall, saying, "The Jester went off on his own. He muttered something about going out into the city..."

Julia followed her uncle to the door and she heard his lie. Turning, she paced back into the library, moving between the shelves, feeling off-balance and afraid. *Uncle lied! Why would he lie? And if the messenger has escorted Lester to the King, then who is this messenger...or...* She stopped short, thinking, *who was that first messenger?*

A summons came to the library; "The King requires Sir Raven and his niece, Julia, to attend him now."

Julia stood, before the King, listening as her uncle repeated, "The jester went off on his own. He said something about going out into the city..."

"And you, Miss Julia? Do you know where he went?" the King asked.

Julia shook her head and answered, "No, Sire." She wanted to tell him what had happened, but felt afraid of her uncle's wrath. Then it washed over her, something was dreadfully wrong.

"Lester has not gone into the city. I know that for sure," the King said, adding, "He's on oath to remain within the palace precincts."

"A messenger, a different one, came for him," Julia blurted.

"He went with the man?"

"Yes, he was coming to finish his visit with you, Sire."

"You saw him leave with this messenger?" the King asked, his gaze upon the curator.

"No, Sire, this is news to me..."

Turning to a captain who waited for orders, the King barked, "I want him found, now! Whatever it takes, however many men, I want you to bring Lester to me before an hour is up!" His gaze moved back to the curator and his niece and he commanded, "You will remain right where you are until Lester is found."

The news was broadcast before the evening meal that a search was being arranged to find the Jester. Even though night had fallen and the air was misty and damp, foot soldiers and mounted guards were out searching. The palace and grounds had been searched thoroughly, twice over, yielding no signs or news of Lester's whereabouts. At midnight, Julia and her uncle were permitted to return to their quarters.

Before sun-up the following day, a reward was posted for news regarding Lester.

The King had an audience with his younger brother, and it resulted in a heated argument. The Crown Prince denied any responsibility for Lester's absence and accused the King of favoring the lad. "I've been dreadfully ill, vomiting, confined to my bedchamber, my aides will tell you, Sire..."

In his small suite of rooms beneath the library, the curator met with his band of cohorts, demanding of them, "Who is this Jester? I thought he was a nothing, a nobody! Kissing my niece, that's what I saw him doing! Well, we can't claim the reward, not one of us! Any of you who narks on me, I'll see you in prison with me. All of you have his blood on your hands. So not a word! It's hard enough keeping my niece from spilling it. And now, if the gossip is right, I should've let him have her. Bastard son of the King, is he? Means he's worth much more than many a man in this place. It's obvious the King favors him."

***

Over a day later, before noon, Lester was carried into the hospice at the palace. Crowds of palace officials, guards and courtiers gathered in groups, discussing the news that Lester the Jester had been found. "More dead than alive," the fore-rider had announced.

King William Henry burst into the hospice chamber where Lester had been taken. He demanded, "What happened to him? How bad is it?"

The captain whose company found Lester, explained, "The doctors are taking care of him and they'll have a prognosis soon, Sire. We believe that the jester has been in the river. A band of travelers found him near the road, six miles downriver. Bound, the ropes still on him. Someone tried to dispose of your jester, Your Majesty. I suggest we keep guards here..."

"Yes, yes, do that. I'll have Chief Alexis investigate. Someone, somewhere in this palace must have seen and known about his bonds, his abduction. What on earth for? Who would want Lester dead?" No one dared to verbalize an answer.

A doctor came from the chamber where Lester lay. "He's awake, Your Majesty. But do not talk too long, he's very weak."

The King sat beside Lester's bed and took his hand, asking, "Who did this, Lester?"

"The river...the rocks."

It was a faint attempt at humor, but the King was not amused. "Who put you there, Lester. Who took you from our palace?"

After a short silence, Lester said, "A group of men, four at least. Either the curator arranged it, Sire, or...but, I'm not sure..."

"Who? Charles...William?"

"I heard a voice, but it sounded like...the curator's...perhaps...but why would *he* want me dead?"

"Why indeed?" the King asked, standing. He brushed his palm on the back of Lester's hand and gave it a squeeze, saying, "Rest and don't worry, you're safe now."

Back in his sanctum, King William Henry sent for his brother and demanded, "Tell me what part *you* had to play in Lester's disappearance, Brother! I want the truth!"

"The truth is, Brother, that I had *nothing* to do with it! I've been laid up, like I feel pain, all over." He saw the doubt on the King's face and bowed his head. "Not that I wouldn't have planned something like it, but you'd not have found him, not if I'd had a part in it! There'd be no trace, not with the vibes I get from that fellow!"

They glared at each other, and the Crown Prince broke the silence by saying, "It's bizarre, Brother. I, who have good reason to rid the world of Lester, did not. Like you, I'd like to know who believed him to be such a threat they wanted to kill him. You know I want Victoria...and he wants that girl in the library..."

"Sire," interrupted the oldest adviser, "Sire, Your Majesty, but you are now able to tell your brother..."

"Tell him?"

"Yes. Your father, the late king wrote in his will that if any of his three sons had life-threatening injuries or illness, then the truth could be told, but not before..."

"*Three* sons?" the crown prince asked, confused.

"Lester is your twin," the King said. "He was named William Lester."

"Twin? He's a year younger!"

"No, he was born some hours after you, Charles. I was there, in the room, though nine years old. Our mother died as he was born. I held you first, then you were taken to Father. Then I held Lester until Father came. He did not look at him, but had eyes and thoughts only for our mother. Then, he turned to me and ranted and raved that Lester had killed her. He allowed Lester to stay in the palace but his birth date was recorded when he was one year and one week old. It was written that Lester's identity be kept as a guarded secret and..."

"But we're not alike..."

"Oh, yes you are. You have your hair long, his is short, but you have the same mannerisms, the same features, you even talk in the same tones..."

"He's shorter, his face is thinner...he's...he's always smiling..."

"You have more reasons to smile than Lester. You should smile much more, Brother."

The pair stared at each other, silent for more than a minute.

"You've complained to me of pain and emotional trauma, every time you're near him..."

Tears welled in the Crown Prince's eyes and his face flushed. He turned on his heel and rushed from the room. He ran up steps and along a corridor, then up to the tallest tower where he went as a lad when he felt frustrated about Lester and his hatred for the gut-wrenching pain he suffered every time he was near him.

Out in the cool air, William Henry raised his hands and shouted, "NO!" Anguish gripped him and he sank to his knees. The years rolled backwards as he recalled the times of agony he knew both he and Lester had shared. William Henry knew that Lester vomited after being berated; he had the same feelings in the pit of his stomach. Weeks, months, years had passed and he had been emotionally tormented; unaware, until now, why.

Standing, he shouted, "Every time I inflicted abuse on him, I felt it! Every time he was angry at me, it made him ill. I should have known! His pain was my pain, and my pain was his..."

Lester surfaced to consciousness feeling foreign affection within his inner being. It felt like the love of a mother, or someone as close. A person sat beside his bed and cradled his hand between two. He sighed. It was like being wrapped in a warm caressing cocoon.

Remembering what had happened, he thought it was the King who sat with him. The King had always cared, in a warm, though distant manner. As he became more lucid, he knew it was not the King, it was someone else, not Julia, not a female. Someone like the King. Perhaps he was dreaming and, in his dream, the form of his father sat with him, whoever his father was... he could not remember. His face was bruised, swollen, and his eyes would not open. The hand tightened on his and as warm wet tears fell on his arm, harmony flooded him. It was a feeling he had never had before nor dared dream would be possible. He sighed again and slept.

King William Henry stepped up behind his brother and placed his hand on the bowed shoulder. Looking up, the crown prince whispered, "The doctors say that he'll recover...but what a mess. You know, Henry, I felt it all, I still feel it. But who would do such a thing?"

The King smiled wryly. His brother had forgotten that he was among those who would have rejoiced at the jester's demise. "It was the curator. He's confessed. He arranged for a band of cohorts to dispose of the threat to his niece's future. He thought he was disposing of a hated, dispensable servant. Now that he knows the truth, well, but then, he's in a cell.

"I'm glad our brother is doing better." The King's eyes were on the Crown Prince. The transformation was utterly incredible.

William Charles bowed his head and said, "We have so much lost time to redeem."

The King had been able to withstand the ranting of his brother William Charles when he had hated his unrecognized twin and he had been able to impart some comfort and solace to Lester, but now, with the two unified, they presented a much more formidable force.

"You kept your promise, Henry," the Crown Prince said, "when Father disallowed you to tell us the truth of our twinship. Well, Lester and I have both made promises, and we should be allowed to keep them."

"You are right," the King replied, "a promise is a promise. And I've promised the ambassador from Jiarya that Princess Cathryn will marry into our family."

***

Bells sounded out across the Capital City. Today was the day. It was to be a triple wedding. The King was marrying Princess Cathryn from Jiarya, William Charles, Crown Prince was wedding his sweetheart, Lady Victoria, who would become that day, 'Crown Princess Victoria'. The newly proclaimed third-in-line to the throne, Prince William Lester, was to marry his chosen love, a library girl, Miss Julia, who would be titled 'Princess Julia'. Not for a century had the throne been so secure within one family.

About the Author:

Carolyn Ann Aish was born Carolyn Ann Gundesen in the small town of Waitara, Taranaki, New Zealand in 1948. She was raised in New Plymouth and now resides in Inglewood beneath the spectacular Taranaki Mountain.

TOMBSTONE WITHOUT A NAME
©2005 by Phillip Lynne

Two men wearing rubber boots pushed through the front gate of Oak Grove Cemetery, shattering the early morning silence. Continuous rain for three days had created miniature lakes among the three hundred tombstones, and stripped the few remaining leaves from the oaks.

"The grave is on the hill in the center," the first man said. "I can see it from my window with binoculars." Jackson Tuttlerow, caretaker of Oak Grove, lived in a small house just outside the gate. Seventy years old, his skin had the color and texture of dark leather, his hair pure white.

Detective Martin Dillon, a head taller and fifty years younger, had blue eyes, brown hair, and wore a gray trench coat. "Have you been up there this morning?"

"No, sir, wanted to wait for you. I watched all night and this morning. No one has been near the grave."

"You're sure about that?"

"There is a fence fifteen feet high with spikes going all the way around the cemetery. Can't see anybody climbing over. Not without a lot of help, that is. And that much help would make noise."

As the two men ascended the hill, they emerged from a slow-moving sea of fog into bright sunshine. Bare oak tree branches rose from the mist as if reaching for the sun's warmth.

"This way," Tuttlerow said, leaving the stone path and making his way through three rows of tombstones. He stopped before a black and white granite tombstone and waited for Dillion.

"There's no name," Dillion observed.

The caretaker nodded. "There was a name there last night. Carved in deep, it was."

Dillion squatted and ran his hand over the tombstone. "Smooth as glass. Could it be a different stone? I mean, somebody could have stayed inside after you locked up last night and switched it."

Tuttlerow seemed offended. "I check the entire cemetery before I lock up. If somebody was hiding in here, I would have found him." He stepped around the tombstone. "Here now, come see this. I wanted to be sure, so I wrote my initials NAT right here in the corner with one of those gold markers that write on anything. I figured not many tombstone switchers would carry a gold marker with them."

"That's a safe bet," Dillion said, glancing around. "No sign of tampering, but there *are* several footprints here. Heavy boots with a criss-cross pattern on the sole."

Tuttlerow held up his left foot. "That is me. Those are from last night when I put my initials on the stone."

Dillion laughed. "I'll take your name off the suspect list." He pinched his lower lip and looked down. "The ground's too soft to hide any other footprints. Okay, guess we can rule out somebody switching the stone, unless they did it by helicopter."

"I would hear a helicopter."

"Of course, you would. On the telephone you said this has happened before?"

"*Two* times this tombstone has been carved with Molly Bircham's name and date of death. Two times I have found the stone next morning with nothing on it."

Dillion nodded. "Okay. Well, the only thing we can do is get it carved again and I'll stakeout the grave."

"I was hoping you would say that," Tuttlerow smiled, heading back for the path. "I will ring Finchers right away. They will call me crazy for having the same stone carved again."

Dillion fell into step with him. "Molly's family must be furious about all this."

"They do not know anything about it. They moved to California same day as the funeral. Poor little girl; dead three weeks and not one of her family come to visit her grave. Something blasphemous about that."

"Why would they move to California and leave Molly here? They could have had a funeral out there."

Tuttlerow shrugged. "Maybe they will ship her body there later?"

"Possible, I suppose. Seems like an awful lot of trouble."

As they went out the front gate, silence returned to the cemetery.

Four nights later, Dillion sat leaning against a large tombstone twenty feet from Molly's grave, a three-foot flashlight and an insulated container of hot cocoa by his side. Stakeouts were nothing new to him, having done more than sixty during his twenty years with the Shortsville Police. This was the first time in a cemetery, however.

Through some optical trick of atmospheric conditions, the moon was enormous and cast eerie shadows from both tombstones and trees. Dillion glanced at the luminous dial of his watch. Eleven-thirty. He slowly stretched his legs to a more comfortable position and inhaled deeply.

Then something moved.

His body went rigid and he focused intently on Molly's tombstone, realizing there had been no sound; he had *sensed* the movement, almost as if the cemetery air had expanded to accommodate a new being.

A young girl was now standing at Molly Bircham's tombstone, her back to him. Her long red hair, a barrette over each ear, fell over a blue-and-white-check patterned dress, and she was wearing light blue ankle socks and black leather shoes.

It was a full minute before Dillion become conscious that,

despite the brightness of the moon, the level of detail he was seeing was not possible. It seemed the girl was emitting her own light from within.

As he stared, the girl dropped to her knees and passed her hand across the tombstone, appearing to be dusting it. She then stood and took a step back.

Dillion found his voice. "Uh, excuse me."

She stiffened, started to turn, then moved quickly around the tombstone.

"Stop, police!" he cried out of habit and immediately felt foolish. "I won't hurt you, little girl!" he added, scrambling to his feet. He switched on the flashlight, sending a wide shaft of light down the hillside. He moved the beam back and forth, revealing nothing but cold, silent tombstones. He pulled a small walkie-talkie from his pocket. "Jackson! Are you there?"

Tuttlerow's voice came back instantly. "I am here."

"A little girl was just here, playing around the tombstone. Have you been watching the gate?"

"Have not taken my eyes off it, sir. And I locked it after you went in."

Dillion lowered the flashlight to the stone, and his blood turned to ice. The half-inch deep engraved letters were gone. "I'm coming down, Jackson," he said, surprised at the sudden quiver in his voice. "Get that gate open!"

Retrieving the container of cocoa, he was aware of something stirring in his chest. A long-forgotten feeling, remembered from childhood, of pounding up darkened basement stairs, panic washing in as unseen monsters strove to prevent him reaching the cellar door. This time, the door was the front gate and the monsters were the residents of Oak Grove Cemetery.

Jackson Tuttlerow said, "The stone was wiped clean by the little girl?"

Dillion was standing at the caretaker's cottage window. The moon, clouds moving across it, silhouetted the hill. "She waved her hand over it and the engraving vanished."

"You could not catch her?"

Dillion turned from the window. "No."

Tuttlerow's eyes narrowed. "There is something bothering you more than a little girl who got away."

Dillion dropped into an overstuffed chair. "I could see her as plain as if it were high noon. She had red hair and was dressed like Dorothy in *The Wizard of Oz*. When I spoke to her, she ran around the tombstone, but now that I think about it, I'm not so sure that she didn't run *through* it."

"Ah, your first experience with a ghost." Tuttlerow smiled. "I see ghosts here all the time. Guess I am used to it. They are all as you describe: every detail as clear as glass even on the darkest night. Congratulations, Detective, you have seen the ghost of Molly Bircham."

Dillion shuddered. "Oh, great."

"There is something wrong with her. Something is preventing her from resting in peace."

"I should dig deeper into Molly's story." Dillion ran a hand over his face. "She gave me quite a scare."

Tuttlerow laughed. "It is the living you should be scared of."

Martin Dillion's office reflected his love for all things ornamental, no matter how cheap or gaudy. A row of stone gargoyles greeted visitors from the desk, while fierce-looking plastic dragons kept watch from atop a bank of filing cabinets. Under the window, a cement cherub water fountain gurgled next to a pot of dirt, home to a pink yard flamingo under a plastic palm tree.

The door opened and Dennis Kelton, Dillion's twenty-two-year-old assistant, entered. "Doesn't it bother you that your workspace resembles a flea market? On a bad day."

Dillion put down his morning coffee. "One man's flea market, another man's eyesore. Can I help it if your taste sucks?"

Kelton smiled. "Okay, okay. I just came in to see how your night went."

Dillion became serious as he related the events in the cemetery.

Kelton stared at him. "A ghost? Are you out of your mind?"

"I'm not sure. For some reason, Molly Bircham doesn't like her tombstone. I know it's crazy. We'll have to handle this one quietly or we'll get tossed in the loony bin."

Kelton was thoughtful, then shrugged. "Okay, so we're investigating ghosts now. What's the first step?"

"Pull the file on Molly Bircham and let's go over the accident. It happened about three weeks ago."

When Kelton came back, he tossed him the manila folder. "What a way to die."

Dillion went through the file, then looked up. "Good God, backing over your own child in the driveway."

"I know. It must be hell knowing you killed your own kid, even if it was an accident."

Dillion pulled his jacket on. "Let's go see the medical examiner."

Jon Effler handed over two steaming coffee mugs. "Molly Bircham? Oh, yeah. The kid that got run over by her father in their driveway."

"Got a picture?" Dillion asked.

"Several, but I don't think you want to see them. She was run over by a pickup truck loaded with firewood. Both left-side tires straight across the head. Do you know what that much weight does to the skull of a twelve-year-old?"

"She died quick?"

"Instantly," Effler replied, pulling open a desk drawer and extracting a folder. "Let me refresh my memory." He flipped quickly through the pages.

"I listed massive head injuries as the cause of death, which is an understatement," he said finally. "There were small stones and some red clay in what used to be her head. I found the same thing on the truck tires. The family had been out gathering wood at Jack

Wright's place all day. Apparently, Molly was tired and fell asleep on the driveway just before her father backed up. I found fibers from her pillow in the mess also."

Dillion shook his head again. "Dear God. Well, we'd best get going, Dennis. We'll drop in at the funeral home."

Effler asked, "Why the interest in this?"

Dillion drained his coffee mug. "Just being curious, as usual."

Wyatt Meager, director of Meager's Chapel, was tall and gaunt with oversized joints, big feet, and a large nose. A thin I'm-sorry-for-your-loss-but-it-puts-bread-on-my-table smile was fixed on his face. His office was a dark, moody room at the back of the funeral home.

"I remember Miss Bircham quite well. A lovely young girl. Brilliant red hair, I recall. Such a shame about her accident."

"Yeah," Dillion said. "Did you work on her?"

"I oversee all preparations of our clients. We have a certain reputation to maintain. The younger employees lack the dedication to carry out the delicate work of preparing the clients for interment without supervision."

"Sure," Dillion said. "Just a bunch of silly kids. Anyway, can you tell me what Molly was buried in?"

Meager's eyes lit up. "I remember it well. Top-of-the-line coffin, trimmed in gold with ivory handles and lined with the finest..."

"Clothes," Dillion interrupted. "What was she wearing?"

"I don't remember *that*. I would have to check my records."

"It's important."

Meager dug through a desk drawer. "Let me see, yes, here it is." The folder was black. "We take pictures of the bodies both before and after preparation. As much a training tool as it is good record keeping. A way of passing on body reconstruction tips to the apprentices."

"You didn't reconstruct Molly did you?"

"Heavens, no. Nothing there to work with. I must warn you, Detective, the pictures are quite graphic and may be offensive to you."

The blood drained from Dillion's face as he studied the first photograph, the "after" picture. The girl's body lay on a padded table, a square block of wood where her head should be, red hair spilling out from underneath. She was wearing a blue and white checked dress, black leather shoes, and light blue ankle socks.

"Dorothy's dress," Dillion said, handing the picture to Kelton.

"I beg your pardon?" Meager asked.

Dillion caught a glimpse of the "before" picture and pushed it back into the envelope. "Nothing. Thank you. We've got the information we came for. Oh, by the way, what was your impression of Oscar and Hilda Bircham?"

"Very caring parents who wanted the best for their unfortunate daughter. I do remember that they were in an unusual hurry, however. They didn't want the normal time for receiving friends and family. We buried Molly in a private, closed coffin ceremony the after day she was brought in."

"Any idea why they were in such a hurry?"

"They were leaving for California, I believe. Something about the father's job being transferred."

Dillion frowned. "Any idea where he worked?"

Meager referenced the folder. "DigiComSat is what he listed on the papers."

"Is there a phone number?"

Meager wrote it on a piece of paper and handed it across. "Is there some trouble here?"

Dillion stood. "Just doing some checking. Thanks again."

Kelton switched off his cellular telephone. "Guess what?"

"Enlighten me."

"Oscar Bircham resigned from DigiComSat three weeks ago."

"He wasn't transferred?"

"Nothing to transfer to. The company has nothing in California. No plans to, either. They did give me a forwarding address and phone number."

Dillion was pinching his lower lip. "So he lied about his being transferred. What type of father skips town the day of his daughter's funeral and lies about the reason?"

"He was in so much grief that he wasn't sure what he was doing?" Kelton ventured.

"No way. I would think it was just the opposite. If he was in so much grief, it would never occur to him to lie about anything. The death of his daughter should have been the overriding concern. Nothing else would matter."

"Okay," Kelton shrugged. "What's next?"

"Back to the office and give this creep a call."

Oscar Bircham asked, "What can I do for you, Detective?"

"I have been going over your case and I had a few questions."

"I wasn't aware that I even had a case."

"Sorry, just cop jargon. My partner and I are doing a follow-up on your daughter's death before closing the files, and need a little light shined on a few things."

"I don't know what I can do, Detective, but I will be more than happy to try."

"The reports say Molly fell asleep behind your pickup truck. How'd that happen?"

"We had been gathering firewood for hours, and Molly, being a very energetic child, was constantly on the move that day. Running here and there, exploring the area, chasing her dog through the trees, things like that. When we returned home, Molly and her mother got out of the truck and went into the house. Or so I thought. My wife *did* go in, but Molly apparently wandered behind the truck with her pillow and lay down on the driveway to sleep."

"She was able to sleep on the hard driveway?"

"Ah, you obviously don't have children, Detective, or you would know that overtired children are able to sleep anywhere, on anything, and in some of the most ridiculous positions."

"How fascinating," Dillion said, rolling his eyes for Kelton's benefit. "Why did you leave town so quickly after the funeral?"

"Business matters required that we move to California."

"What business matters?"

"I was being transferred."

"Strange," Dillion said. "We spoke to DigiComSat just today and they said you resigned."

The line was silent for two seconds. "You misunderstand, Detective. My *new* job required me to be transferred to California. I have started a computer consulting firm of my own."

Dillion frowned. "You couldn't do that here?"

"You have to go where the action is. Uh, I really must ask your forgiveness now, Detective, but I have a full plate today. It's still mid-morning here, you know."

Dillion tried to sound gracious. "I think we can lay this case, uh, file to rest now. Have a good day." He hung up and said, "He stinks like rotten cheese."

"What do you mean?" Kelton asked.

"He was too cool, too matter-of-fact, and he got flustered when I called his bluff about being transferred."

"Maybe it's time we check him out on the computer."

"Yes, let's."

Hershel Murphey, a twenty-five-year-old computer geek with thick glasses and wild blonde hair, oversaw the police computer department with a direct link to the National Police Net.

His looked up as his door opened. "What are you doing here, Dillion? I thought you didn't trust computers."

"In the right hands, I guess they serve a purpose. I need you to run a check on a guy."

"That's what I'm here for. What's the name?"

Dillion told him. Murphey's fingers became a blur on the keyboard, the computer monitor flashing. "Here he is."

Dillion read quickly. "Busted three times for assault and battery. Two acquittals, one fine. Good God, he punched out a priest!"

Dennis Kelton pointed, "And look, he moved each time. The first one was in Texas, the second in North Carolina, and the third in Tennessee."

"Now his daughter gets killed and he splits to California."

"There's more," Murphey said, scrolling the computer screen down to a picture of Molly Bircham. "Cute kid. Hey, the *related files* button is enabled. Want to see?"

"Sure," Dillion said.

The screen faded, then brightened, revealing a second picture of Molly in which she appeared somewhat younger with her hair done up in a tight bun.

"Hello, what's this?" Dillion asked, leaning forward. "Looks like Molly, but it says her name is Suzannah Stevens."

Murphey's experienced eyes scanned the screen. "This file was accessed because Suzannah's physical description matches that of Molly's, almost exactly. But, Suzannah's address is in North Carolina and Molly is local."

Dillion started. "Suzannah was kidnapped three weeks ago from the Wilton Home for Children!"

Kelton looked up. "Molly died three weeks ago."

Dillion began pacing. "What are the odds of two girls who look almost exactly alike and living hundreds of miles apart, making headlines at the same time?"

"Almost impossible," Murphey said.

"That's what I thought. Dennis, we're taking a trip to North Carolina." Dillion thumped Murphey's back. "You've been an incredible help, Hershel, put yourself down for a raise and a promotion."

"Yeah, like you could do anything about either one."

The Wilton Home for Children was a Victorian-style house given to the city of Wilton in 1950 by the illustrious Rothfield family. The administrator, Henrietta Beatty, met Dillion and Kelton at the front door, dressed in a startling black dress and pearls, her silver hair done up in braids held in place by delicate gold combs. A pair of reading glasses perched on her tiny nose.

"Detectives Dillion and Kelton?" she asked in a smooth voice.

"The same."

"Do come in." She held the door wide, then led them to a stylish office on the second floor. "I can have tea sent up."

"Thank you, no," Dillion said. "Let's get right to it. What can you tell us about Suzannah Stevens?"

Her eyes misted over and she produced a lace handkerchief. "Such a delightful young lady. An angel. Good manners, respectful, intelligent. Her parents were killed five years ago when a train struck their car. She was in the vehicle, but received only minor injuries. As you can imagine, she required several months of intense therapy."

Dillion smiled. "She came out of it okay?"

"Oh, yes. She was very well adjusted. You couldn't ask for a better child."

"I'm surprised no one has adopted her," Kelton mused.

"That's one of the great mysteries of my job, Detective. She would be the perfect addition to any family. The lack of interest weighs on her, too. I can tell. If only that nice couple would have followed through a few weeks ago."

"Someone tried to adopt Suzannah recently?" Dillion asked.

"Oh, yes. Phelps, I believe was the name. They spent two days with her, visiting the lighthouses and the beach."

"What happened?"

"I don't know. They suddenly decided against going any further. No real reason given. Suzannah was devastated. She disappeared that night. We thought at first that she had run away, but she left her teddy bear and she was never without it. It was a gift from her parents, you see."

"You told the local police about these two people?"

"Oh, of course. They tried to find them, but they gave us a false address."

Dillion leaned forward. "Give me a description of Mr. Phelps."

"Oscar was about six feet tall, two hundred pounds, brown hair, brown eyes, with a mustache."

Dillion almost choked. "*Oscar*?"

Dennis Kelton retrieved a photo from his briefcase. "Take a look at this photo, Ms. Beatty and..."

"That's him!" she gasped. "He looks different here, but that's him. And that's Hilda Phelps standing next to him. But she had black hair then, instead of the blonde in this picture. Who are these people, Detective?"

"Oscar and Hilda Bircham," Dillion said. "We've been doing some investigating concerning their daughter who was killed in an accident three weeks ago, about the time Suzannah disappeared. Come on, Dennis, let's get going."

She escorted them to the front door. "Please let me know as soon as you find out something about Suzannah. We're all at our wit's end since she disappeared."

Dillion took her hand. "We'll let you know the moment something happens, I promise."

In the car, Kelton was thinking aloud. "So, we know Bircham is involved in both cases. But how do Molly and Suzannah fit in? One dies in an accident and the other has been kidnapped. What's the connection here?"

"It is a mystery," Dillion agreed. "We can account for only one of the girls. Molly is buried in Oak Grove. Where is Suzannah?"

"Think the Birchams took her to replace Molly? Like a substitute daughter?"

"Looks that way, doesn't it? Get out the file. What was Molly's death date?"

"Effler got her on September thirty."

"And Suzannah vanished when?"

"The, uh, twenty-ninth."

"That kills the substitute theory. You wouldn't get a substitute daughter *before* you know you need one. Unless you knew ahead of time that you'd be needing one. Besides, everybody knows that Molly died. Her own father actually wrote her obituary in the local paper. How would it look if all of a sudden his dead daughter's out playing in the front yard?"

Kelton snapped his fingers. "That's why they bugged out for California. Nobody out there would know about the accident. They could have a daughter out there and nobody would think anything was strange."

Dillion was thoughtful. "True, but we're forgetting Suzannah. *She* would have a problem with it. Nothing would get more attention than a kid running around yelling she'd been kidnapped."

Kelton nodded. "Unless they told her they adopted her legally?"

"Then she'd be wondering why they took her without her being allowed to say goodbye to Ms. Beatty and she'd want her teddy bear."

Kelton nodded again. "Okay, so where are we in all this?"

Dillion frowned. "We've still got one girl missing, one in a grave, and..."

Kelton looked at him. "What is it?"

"The girl in the grave. What if she's not Molly?"

"Huh?"

"What if Suzannah is in the grave?"

"Whoa, boss, you're getting out there."

"Think about it! Two girls as identical as you can get. Who would know the difference?"

"The Medical Examiner would, wouldn't he? I mean, surely positive ID was established?"

"What for?" Dillion was shouting now, pushing the accelerator to the floor. "Molly Bircham died in an accident. Pure and simple. Oscar Bircham himself would have made the positive ID for the ME's office."

"So, we're going with the assumption that the Bircham's took Suzannah?"

"They were in disguise, had different names, went nuts over Suzannah, and you still don't believe they took her?"

"Okay. Let's say it *was* Suzannah that was buried. How, then, did her head get destroyed? Molly was the one who was run over."

"Ah, the rub here is, are we sure Molly was run over? Can you at least admit that the body in Oak Grove *might* be Suzannah?"

Kelton was silent for a minute. "Okay, yeah, I'll agree to the possibility that it might be Suzannah. But I still have to ask: why?"

"Beats me," Dillion said. "We need to pay a visit to the Birchams."

"How are you going to justify a trip to California? The brass won't like it."

"This one's on me," Dillion said. "First flight Friday after work. We can be back by Sunday afternoon."

"You must be really sure of this."

"I am," Dillion said. Then added, "I think."

It was Saturday afternoon when Dillion stopped the rental car in front of a nondescript house outside Weed, California.

Hilda Bircham answered the door and Dillion put on the charm. "Hello. Would Oscar be home by any chance? I really must speak with him."

"He's not here right now."

Dillion feigned desperation. "Oh, dear, it really is most important."

She stepped out onto the porch. "Would you like to wait for him? He should be along any minute." She led them to a white plastic picnic table under a picture window. "Can I get you some iced tea?"

Dillion sat down. "No thanks, I'm fine."

"Me too," Kelton said.

Dillion looked around. "It's so quiet here. You must not have children?"

She studied the tabletop. "Children? No. No children. How do you know my husband?"

"We knew each other in Shortsville."

The effect on Hilda was immediate and severe, her head jerking up, her eyes wide. "Shortsville?"

Dillion flipped his police identification. "Martin Dillion, Hilda, detective with the Shortsville Police. This is Detective Dennis Kelton."

"What do you want?"

"To speak to your husband," Dillion said. "About Molly."

A car pulled in the driveway and Oscar Bircham got out and approached the porch. "What's going on?"

Dillion got to his feet, flashing his ID again. "Detective Martin Dillion, Shortsville Police. We spoke on the phone a few days ago."

Bircham sat next to his wife and put an arm around her. "If you have more questions, why didn't you just call?"

"I, uh, like the face-to-face thing much better."

Bircham shrugged. "What would you like to talk about?"

"Suzannah Stevens."

The reactions of the two Birchams were exactly opposite. While Oscar remained calm, a slight smile fixed to his lips, Hilda gasped and brought a hand to her mouth, her eyes wide.

"Who?" Oscar asked.

"The young girl you spent time with on the Outer Banks three weeks ago. Don't remember? Maybe the memories were discarded along with the disguises and the name Phelps."

"How did . . ." Hilda started.

"Shut up!" Oscar hissed. "You're way out of your jurisdiction, Dillion."

Dillion leaned back and crossed his legs. "You're right, of course. That's why I brought along some local help." He jerked a thumb over his shoulder.

A Crown Victoria was just pulling into the driveway. A man and a woman stepped out and came to the house. Both wore business suits, badges prominent on their jacket lapels.

"Detective William Conners, *local* fuzz," the man said, turning off a small walkie-talkie, the twin of which Dillion now placed on the table. Connors was over six feet tall with crew cut brown hair, the look of boxer about him.

"Marion Canton," the woman said, her blue eyes shining

beneath shoulder-length blond hair. "Good afternoon."

"Been hearing some strange things about you two," Conners said. "My interest is piqued, so you can either answer Detective Dillion's questions, or you can answer mine."

Bircham had the look of a hunted animal. "Not without a lawyer."

"You think you need one?" Dillion asked.

"No, it's just that I don't like police harassment at my own home."

Conners laughed. "Let's take a walk, Bircham." It was not a request. "You can tell me all about it."

Oscar hesitated and glanced at his wife. Something passed between them. Conners then took him by the arm they left the porch.

Marion Canton pulled a notepad from her pocket. "Ready when you are, Detective Dillion."

Dillion smiled at Hilda. "Tell us about Suzannah."

"What do you want to know?" she asked. Her fingers were in motion, playing across the top of the table, folding and unfolding. "She was a beautiful little girl."

"Just like your Molly, right? They could have been twins."

Tears welled in her eyes. "Yes. Just like Molly."

"Why the Phelps charade?"

"That was Oscar's idea. He's into that sort of thing: pretending to be someone he's not. He gets a thrill out of it."

"He gets a thrill from kidnapping, too?" Dillion asked.

"I don't know what you mean."

"You don't know that Suzannah has disappeared? I think you do, but I'm not going to argue with you. Not yet. But, let me tell you something else you don't know. There is a little girl wandering around in Oak Grove Cemetery wiping her tombstone clean whenever Molly's name is carved into it."

Hilda Bircham was clearly stunned. "What?"

"That's right. A ghost, if you can believe it. I spent the night in the cemetery and saw her myself. She's determined we know that

Molly's name doesn't belong."

Hilda broke down, sobbing into her hands. "Dear God, that poor girl!"

Dillion handed across a handkerchief. "Tell us what happened, Hilda."

"He'll kill me if I do," she said in a whisper.

"I think the secret is already doing that," Kelton said.

A small group of men were gathered in the trees at the back of Wright's farm. Jack Wright himself was wielding a shovel, forcing the blade into the cold, hard ground. Jon Effler stood to one side, the medical records of Molly Bircham under his arm. Dillion and Kelton stood beside him, their collars turned up against the cold wind.

"God, I hate this part of it," Dillion said.

Behind them, another man was making his way through the trees. In his late fifties, Captain Walter Johnson was not happy to be out on such a day.

"Morning, Walt," Dillion called.

"Dillion. Mr. Kelton," Johnson stopped next to them. "Have we found her yet?"

Dillion shook his head. "Not yet."

"While we're waiting, Dillion, why don't you fill me in?"

And Dillion did, starting with the appearance of the girl in the cemetery through the trip to California.

"Hilda cracked like an egg when we told her about Suzannah's unrest. She finked out her husband in a heartbeat. Oscar Bircham, you see, likes to punch on people smaller than him to relieve tension. He has used her as a punching bag more than once, so she was happy to tell all.

"Seems Oscar was going ballistic over something and took one of his shotguns into the backyard, where he proceeded to blast away at birds, squirrels, anything that moved. Then, when living targets became scarce, he decided to pump a dozen or so shots into an old tree house in the yard. Unfortunately, Molly had hid there when he started blowing his top. She was hit several times in the chest and stomach. Bircham knew she was in there only when blood started dripping through the tree house floor."

"My God," Johnson said.

"Molly took over an hour to die. The bastard let her go out on an old cat blanket in the basement, if you can believe that."

"Where was the wife when all this was happening?"

"Shopping. Oscar told her about Molly when she returned that evening. They decided to hide their daughter's death; Hilda, because she was scared to death of Oscar, Oscar because he already had record of violent assaults. There was just no way he could claim he accidentally shot his daughter."

"So, where does the other girl come in?"

Kelton spoke up. "A family friend in North Carolina called them in August after seeing a television report on the Wilton Home For Children. During the report, there was a close-up on Suzannah Stevens, who looked exactly like Molly Bircham. So, after Molly died, Oscar and Hilda disguised themselves, used the name Phelps, and went to check her out. She was a perfect match. They kidnapped her, brought her back here, and concocted what they thought was the perfect story."

Dillion continued, "After bringing Suzannah to Shortsville, Oscar knocked her out with a piece of the firewood and laid her down behind the pickup. He was careful to put Molly's pillow under her head in case someone decided to do a fiber analysis. Then he backed over her head, erasing any identifying features.

"It was pretty smart. They could admit they accidentally killed their daughter, produce her body, and still come off looking like victims of a tragic sequence of events. Burying Molly out here was a stroke of genius also. Their story was that they had spent the day here gathering firewood. Traces of dirt from this area were found in the shattered remains of Suzannah's head. So, in coming here, they disposed of Molly's body *and* picked up the dirt on the tires in case anybody checked."

Johnson shook his head. "The tenth level of hell is reserved for people like this."

At that moment, Jack Wright shouted, "Detective Dillion! I think we've found something."

The policemen moved to the dig and watched as an object wrapped in black plastic was lifted from the hole. Jon Effler stepped forward, cut a long slit in the plastic, and opened it gently. There was a flash of red as the girl's hair caught the wind and swirled around and over her face.

Effler stood after examining the body. "It is Molly Bircham," he said in a low voice. "I'm positive this time." There was a hint of regret in his voice.

Dillion put his hand on Effler's back. "Get her to your car, Jon. We'll go on and exhume Suzannah and meet you back at your office."

It took less than two hours to remove Suzannah's coffin from Oak Grove Cemetery.

Two days later, Jackson Tuttlerow stood in front of two newly engraved tombstones. He smiled when he saw that both still had the correct information. He placed a basket of flowers between them, said a silent prayer, and then walked back down the hill.

About the author:

Phillip Lynne lives in Knoxville, Tennessee, and describes himself as "a maniac with a word processor." He has had a few items published, both in print and on the Internet; and has won a writing award or two in his time.